WOLF BORN

SHIFTER PARANORMAL ROMANCE

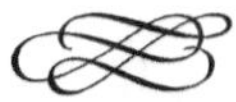

ANN GIMPEL

Edited by
ANGELA KELLY
Illustrated by
FIONA JAYDE

CONTENTS

WOLF BORN

UNDERGROUND HEAT, BOOK TWO

By
Ann Gimpel

Shifters keep their friends close and their enemies closer in a dark, gritty world where passion flares hot and sweet.

COPYRIGHT PAGE

BOOK DESCRIPTION, WOLF BORN

Shifters keep their friends close and their enemies closer in a dark, gritty world where passion flares hot and sweet.

Max leads a double life in a futuristic California that's almost out of resources. Despite grave risks, he ran for state governor to protect his people. He's also leader of the shifter underground. Threatened with genocide, many shifters have gone into hiding. Some blame Max and the underground for their plight, rather than the governmental edict that's meant death for so many.

Audrey works for Max. Unlike most humans with low levels of shifter blood who bless their lucky stars they avoided the purge, she wants to be a shifter. If she could find a way to finesse it, she'd quit her job in a heartbeat and go to work helping the shifter underground. The only sticking point is Max. She's been half in love with him forever.

Against a dog-eat-dog political backdrop where no one knows who their allies are, Max and Audrey spar with one another. Max fears she's part of the group trying to kill him. Audrey has no idea about Max's double identity and worries she won't be able to walk away from their fiery attraction to help the underground.

After a second attempt on his life, Max faces critical choices. Will he follow his head or his heart?

This book is a beautiful story of two people meant for each other who simply have to learn to believe and trust. Each other. Themselves. Fate. To stand up for what they believe in and want and NEED. It's the story of love and what family—human and pack— can accomplish when they work together. A very enjoyable 4.5 **** star read. I look very much forward to book 3 and I am pretty sure any other books Ann Gimpel writes—especially shifters—will find its way onto my Kindle.

I loved Wolf Born. Audrey and Max have smoking hot chemistry. Max is the Governor of California and the head of the shifter underground. He'd been attracted to his secretary Audrey but she isn't his mate...or is she? The fact she works for him complicates matters, of course.

I've read a lot of shifter romance and Ann Gimpel's Wolf Born is my new favorite. It might have been love at first sight for Max and Audrey but it wasn't mate at first sight. Perfect. This series just keeps getting better as the struggle of the shifter underground continues! As a history buff I love the parallels between the shifter underground and the Underground Railroad.

The story was an interesting one, that had some great futuristic technology. I enjoyed the things the author came up with for the future. The explosive way Max and Audrey come together is sexy, sweet, and so loving! This was my first time reading this author and I have already looked up more of her work and can't wait to read it. If you want a sexy shifter story that has some things you haven't read about before then this is for you!

A brilliant follow up to Roman's Gold, I love the futuristic setting of these books, it's a fresh spin on the shifter tale. I like that Kate and Devon from the first book put in an appearance, I loved their story so it was nice to read more from them. I really enjoyed reading the Underground Heat series and hope there will be more...maybe Johannes story?

I found this to be an enjoyable read and totally unlike any other shifter book I have read. Ms. Gimpel set the scene really well as the possibility of our planet running out of resources is a real issue even today. This isn't an easy throwaway read as I feel the issues raised will resonate for many. Yes it's a paranormal romance but it's much more than that. This is a book to awaken minds and the enticing characters are sure to delight. I would rate this a 5 as I found I didn't put it down until I had finished!

CHAPTER 1

Maximillian Sigayev loped up the steps two at a time as he moved from the bottom floor of the shifter underground safe house to the hovercraft port on its roof. He could have taken the elevator but he'd be cooped up in the aircraft for an hour. Any exercise was better than none. He caught himself whistling and grinned as he curved his fingers around the ritual mating stone buried deep in his pocket. It had been a pleasure to join Kate Roman and Devon Heartshorn in the traditional ceremony. He'd have to return to complete the ritual once the wound in Devon's side was completely healed, and he could shift again.

The part of the ceremony that had yet to occur was Kate and Devon's animals mating, while Max looked on to bless their union.

Max laid his palm on the glass plate next to the door that opened onto the roof. It beeped softly, and the locking mechanism released. Ever cautious, Max sent his lupine senses swirling outward to make certain no one lay in wait for him. Breath whistled from between his teeth. Up until now he'd been very lucky. His double life was bound to catch up to him.

"For God's sake, find us a mate before your penchant to take risks does us in," his wolf side growled.

"You've been pretty quiet," Max observed, not wanting to engage in a discussion about mated ones. It wasn't as if he could simply look on the vid feed or place an ad. Shifters were persona non grata. No one admitted to having more than fifty percent shifter blood—if they wanted to live.

"That's because I'm smart enough to shut up unless I have something important to say."

"We can talk once we're airborne."

"It's safe. I already checked." His wolf's tone held a supercilious edge as it frequently did.

Max trusted his wolf, but he still peered cautiously around the barely cracked door. His silver hovercraft gleamed in the morning sun. Walls rose around it on all sides to shield the safe house roof from casual eyes below. While all that brick made landing in high winds a little tricky, the added safety was worth it. Satisfied, Max strode forward, unlocked the craft's door by depressing a button on his wrist computer, and settled into the pilot's seat.

Even that quick glance at his computer showed over a hundred voice and text messages. Max growled. He hadn't been particularly forthcoming about his whereabouts when he left Sacramento the previous night. Employing a bit of shifter magic, he'd snuck away like a cat burglar. No one liked it when they couldn't find him.

He engaged the onboard generator. The craft sputtered and moved upward as soon as the electric motor developed enough torque. Getting it out of the Berkeley city airspace unobserved would be a trick-and-a-half. As California's governor, he had latitude in terms of the air quality laws, but he didn't like to flaunt his power. He set a course due east, past Hayward, to get him beyond the Bay Area corridor and over the foothills as soon as possible. Once there, he'd turn north.

He'd just settled in to review messages when his wolf snarked, *"I thought you were going to talk with me once we were underway."*

"Look." Max kept his mind-voice mild. *"I'd like to find our mated one just as much as you. We don't spend much time with shifters."*

"You always have excuses. There will be a lot more of us once everyone gets dosed with that serum."

Max pursed his lips. The wolf had a point. The intravenous infusion developed by law enforcement scientists to give cops an edge sniffing out shifters had actually pushed the ones with more than ten percent blood to full-blown shifter status. Thanks to quick thinking on Kate Roman's part, the serum was now in the underground's hands and being parceled out to strengthen and swell their ranks.

"Now you're the one who's quiet," his wolf persisted.

"Sorry. Just thinking."

"That's the problem. You think too much. Shifter partner or not, do you even remember the last time we had sex—with something other than your hand, that is?"

"Point taken. I do not want to talk about this. I have things to do."

"Finding a mate for us will never happen if you don't prioritize it." The wolf hesitated. Max hoped he was done, but he went on, *"Kate's mountain cat had to tell her Devon was her special one. She would've missed it, otherwise."* The contemptuous undercurrent was back in spades.

Max clamped his jaws together. One of the problems with these conversations was they reminded him how desperately under-fucked he was. Ever since the U.S. government had decreed shifters were to be imprisoned—or killed outright—two years before, he'd kept to himself. Before that, he'd been extremely selective, limiting his amorous escapades to other shifters since human women rarely turned him on. In his two hundred and twenty years, he'd never come across his mated one. Not that he'd looked very hard, but there weren't many candidates, either.

He grimaced. The wolf wasn't far wrong about his tendency to bury himself ass over teakettle in work. Max liked tasks where he could tweak the probability of success in his favor. Finding a mate had always seemed as unlikely as spinning flax into gold. Because he hadn't liked the odds, he'd focused his attention elsewhere.

He glanced out the hovercraft window and punched a course correction into the onboard computer system. He'd be back in the state's capitol in about half an hour. No point in antagonizing his wolf, particularly when he was probably right. *"Once we get to the other side of this war, you have my word I'll work on finding us a mate."*

The wolf subsided into snarls, apparently done with trying to convince Max of anything.

"It's not an empty promise," Max added.

"Talk is cheap."

Max snorted and bit back a laugh. *No shit.* If he had a nickel for every slick line he heard from the politicians in Sacramento, he'd be a rich man. He switched his focus to his wrist computer and attacked the message stack, texts first, then voice. By the time he landed at the hovercraft port atop his building in the state's capitol, security was waiting for him, ringed around the landing pad.

He stepped from the craft, reached in to grab his computer and briefcase, and straightened. "What?" He leveled a glance at the half dozen guards. "You're unhappy I ran off and left, and now you're going to dog me so it doesn't happen again?"

"That's about the size of it, boss." Loren, the lead security expert, sauntered forward, his lean six-foot frame encased in an immaculately pressed uniform. Dark hair was shaved close to his head. Shrewd blue eyes didn't miss much. It looked like he wanted to snap off a salute and was holding himself back.

"My office will be much too crowded with all of you in it. Once we get there, you'll need to draw straws to see who guards the door."

"You got it, boss," another guard with a blond crew cut said.

"Glad you're back," Loren offered. "It would have, ah, looked bad if something had happened and none of us even knew where you were."

Max winced at the censure in the man's voice. Loren was trying to do a job, and Max wasn't making it very easy for him. He let his gaze settle briefly on each man. "While I understand your concern, I will not be a prisoner. I appreciate that you take my safety very seriously. Believe it or not, so do I. This job is hard enough without feeling like I can't even take a crap without an audience." He pushed past the group, opened the door into the building, and walked briskly down the hall, knowing they'd follow him.

His office was at the very end of the corridor. He spoke a word so the voice-activated electronic lock would open. With one hand on the latch, he turned. "Have someone fly my hovercraft back to my house. The activation codes are in your files. Two of you at a time outside my office. No more unless there's some special public event."

He closed his door on the chorus of, *Yes, sirs* and shook his head. He'd had to pull shifter magic—and leave from his home in the middle of the night—to escape his watchdogs. With the uptick in violence, they were fiercely protective of him. Too much so for comfort.

"You could quit," the wolf commented.

Max nodded thoughtfully. *"Yeah, I could, but we need the power of this office to make sure shifters can walk free again. Between this and heading up the shifter underground, it feels like I'm living on borrowed time. These double life things have a way of imploding."*

"For once, I agree with you. What are you waiting for? Get to work."

When Max looked away from the wall screen, light was fading from the room. He'd set *Do Not Disturb* flags on every electronic account to ensure uninterrupted time to consider legislation, e-sign critical documents, and make a dent in the never-ending cavalcade of petitions from legislators. Reluctantly, he took down the flags and waited for the onslaught. It came almost immediately with a knock on the door.

"Enter."

The door flew open. Audrey, a tall, leggy, strawberry blonde with hazel eyes, charged into the room. At five-feet-ten, she was only a few inches shorter than him. As usual, her long hair was drawn into a severe bun that accentuated the exotic Slavic bone structure in her face. Her tailored black suit hugged considerable curves and exposed a lot of leg. She'd come with the job when he won the election eighteen months before and was as close to a personal assistant as he had.

Over those months, Max had expended a lot of energy not focusing on her full breasts, slender waist, and rounded rump. Today wasn't any different, and he dragged his gaze reluctantly from her perfect body.

"Sir." Barely concealed reproach danced beneath her words. "I've been waiting for you to take down your privacy curtain." She may as well have yelled at him for getting in the way of her doing her job.

"Tell me what you need." He quirked a brow, considered telling her he wasn't in the mood for her jibes, but bit back the words. She was a hell of a fine-looking woman. It always defused his ill-humor. Sexual tension simmered in the air between them, all the more palpable because he forced himself to ignore it.

"Where do you want all this?" She jiggled a large stack of documents.

He rolled his eyes. "Why are you carting paper around? Why not have someone scan them and e-send them to me? For that fact, why weren't they electronic in the first place?"

She shook her head. "These need immediate attention. They're really, really, uh, sensitive. If someone—"

"If we don't have a secure vid feed hookup here, then nowhere is safe. Dump them over there. I'll get to them tonight."

She put the stack where he'd pointed and balanced from one high-heeled foot to the other. He stared at shapely calves disappearing into stocking-clad thighs and then forced his eyes back to her face.

"Um, I was wondering if…" Her voice ran down. She started over. "See, you've been in here all day, and—"

"Whatever it is, Audrey, just spit it out. Obviously—" he gestured toward the foot high stack of reading material she'd just offloaded "—I'm far from done for the day."

Color stained her fair face. In a flash of insight, Max knew what she wanted and was sorry he'd pushed her.

"She wants sex. I smell it." The wolf chortled.

"I can't fuck her. She works for me."

"Who made that rule?"

"Is something wrong, sir?" Audrey looked at him oddly.

"Nothing at all. Why?"

"I don't know. You just got this faraway look in your eyes for a moment. It was as if part of you wasn't here anymore." The color in her face deepened. "Sorry. That didn't come out quite right. It's really none of my business."

"You never did tell me what you wanted to say." Max softened his voice. She truly was a stunning woman. Single, too, after a long, drawn-out divorce.

"Well." She studied the carpet embossed with the State Seal. "You have to eat dinner some time. I was thinking we could catch a bite and then come back, and I'll walk you through what's in those documents. I wasn't sure I should read them, but I'd already begun —" she shrugged, looking uncomfortable "—and so, I just finished them."

"Not a problem. You had to qualify for a top secret security clearance to work as my administrative assistant."

The edges of her mouth twitched into half a smile. "Funny, but it's the same thing I told myself."

"Dinner is an excellent idea." Max managed a smile. He didn't really want to take a break but saw the wisdom in an hour away from the unending flow of work. Sitting across a small, intimate table from Audrey held undeniable appeal too.

First, he needed to check on the underground. No one had messaged him for hours, and he was worried about them.

Crap! It's because I had the flags up.

Audrey had blasted through the door within seconds of him taking them down, so he hadn't had a chance to check the special scrambled feed on his wrist computer. He pushed to his feet. "Tell you what. Give me a minute to throw cold water on my face and wash up. I'll meet you at your desk."

The smile she shot him could've lit an entire city. "I'll make us reservations somewhere. Do you have a preference?"

He thought for a moment. "Sure. Call the Schenectady Steakhouse. They have sound-shielded rooms. We can bring your document pile with us and kill two birds with one stone."

Her smile faded a few lumens. "Of course, sir. I'll just gather them up—" She took a step toward the file folders.

He waved her away. "Never mind. I'll bring them with me."

Max breathed a sigh of relief when the door closed behind her. He hoped she didn't have ulterior motives, or at least, if she did, that she'd be subtle enough to keep them under wraps. He didn't want to have to tell Audrey he found her attractive, but—

"If she wants us, we should fuck her," his wolf yapped from the sidelines.

"What? You've lowered your standards. She's not a shifter."

"She has some shifter blood. I scented it."

"Yes, well so did I, but not enough to turn into anything."

"So give her some of that serum, and see what happens," the wolf suggested snidely.

"Hush. Let me see how the rest of us are doing."

Max clicked buttons on his wrist computer and scanned messages from the safe house he'd left that morning. The group of cops was assimilating well. There'd been some problems with one man's wife. She wasn't thrilled to be married to a bear, even one who promised he'd spend as much time in his human form as he could.

Kate and Devon thanked him for marrying them. He clicked a quick, *You're welcome*, still feeling warm and fuzzy from having conducted their mating ceremony. Both mountain lion shifters, they made a strong couple.

In just a few minutes, he set the computer to standby. Thank Christ there weren't any pressing issues that required his immediate attention.

He trotted to the restroom that opened off the back of his office, splashed water on his face, and rinsed his hands. Strands of hair had escaped the queue he habitually wore. Max pulled the elastic band, re-secured his shoulder-length blond hair, and tucked it beneath his suit jacket. The blue eyes that stared back at him in the mirror looked tired. He rubbed them, but it only made them more bloodshot. A quick rummage through a drawer produced eye drops.

By the time he scooped up the stack of paperwork, locked his office, and headed for Audrey's desk one floor down, he felt downright chipper. Waiting for him, bag slung over a shoulder, she held out her arms. "Here. Give me some of those."

"Nah. They're not heavy. Did you get us reservations?"

She nodded. "They weren't busy. It's only a couple of blocks. Would you like to walk?"

"Not a bad idea—" he began.

"Nope." The security officer du jour's voice rang from behind them. "We're driving you."

Max turned and raised a curious eyebrow. "Why? I was only gone for a few hours this morning. What the hell happened around here?"

The security officer blew out a tense breath. "Ever since things blew up at the Berkeley cop shop, criminals here have gone wild. Guess they're anticipating things will go south here too."

"Have they?" Max held his breath, secretly rooting for an infusion of more shifters to fight for the cause.

"Not yet, but that whole serum thing could blow up on us just like it did in Berkeley. Law enforcement here was a little behind the eight ball. Didn't start taking it until about ten days ago—"

"It's one of the things that's in all those documents," Audrey interrupted. "Once we sit down, I can fill you in."

"Okay. Let's get moving." Max met the security officer's brown gaze. "Sorry—" he eyed the man's badge, "—O'Hare. You must be new."

"Yes, sir."

"Where's the officer working with you?"

The man looked momentarily startled. "Uh, what other officer, sir?"

"Didn't Loren agree there'd be two of you at all times? I distinctly remember him acquiescing to that plan when he showed up with six of you this morning, and I felt stampeded."

"If he did, sir, no one told me. Would you like me to ring for another guard?"

Max thought about it. The extent of the security around him was ridiculous. "No. We're fine. I assume we're heading for the garage."

"That would be correct, sir."

Max gestured at Audrey to go ahead of him. They walked to the elevator, waited, and rode it down several levels toward the parking garage. Max's sensitive nose twitched. The guard smelled...odd. Fear sweat. Surely things weren't so desperate in downtown Sacramento that the man would be afraid.

Running on instincts that had rarely failed him, Max pushed the *Stop Car* button. He whirled to face O'Hare. The man's face turned white. "What are you doing, sir?"

"I'm not certain. Hand over your identification."

The guard patted his back pockets. A frantic look washed over his face, but it was gone in an instant. "Don't seem to have my wallet with me, sir. I must've left it upstairs. Maybe on your secretary's desk." He smiled weakly.

"Fine." Max pushed the button to return them to the building's next-to-the-top floor. "You can retrieve it. Audrey, text the security company. Ask them if they've ever heard of this guy."

As they neared the top floor, the odor rolling off the guard intensified: aggression mixed with fear. "I want you in front of me," Max snapped. "Now."

O'Hare—if that was really his name—lunged. Max was ready and heaved the stack of papers right at him. Audrey bit back a scream. She sounded like a hissing kettle.

O'Hare's brown eyes blazed hatred. "You're a shifter," he snarled. "Dirty, fucking traitor." He sidestepped the paper blizzard and grabbed his gun.

The elevator door opened. Audrey didn't wait for instructions. She dove through it and raced for her desk. Max judo chopped O'Hare's gun hand. The weapon clattered to the elevator's tile floor, and Max kicked it half way across the room. He engaged the button to close the elevator's door, trapping them inside. Max needed privacy. This was as good a way as any to get it.

O'Hare threw himself at Max, teeth bared. Max grappled with him and drove a knee into the man's groin. O'Hare grunted and doubled over with pain. Max linked to his supernatural shifter strength and delivered a blow to the fake security guard's neck designed to sever his spinal column. Breathing hard, he stood watch over the body until he was certain the man was dead.

It hadn't been a contest. Not really. He'd never been in any real danger. His identity was a much bigger problem than O'Hare's feeble attack. Max engaged the elevator to take him back to Audrey's level. He'd been compromised. The only question was how many people knew about him.

Christ! What the fuck do I do next?

CHAPTER 2

The elevator door whooshed open on Audrey, standing in a shooter's stance clutching a highly illegal laser stun pistol. Much of her hair had escaped its bun, and spots of color rode high on both cheeks. She looked so captivating, it took his breath away. He could almost imagine her head thrown back, neck corded with passion as she shrieked her delight at all the things he could do to pleasure her. He blinked hard and refocused. Death was licking at his heels. Now was not the time to indulge in sexual fantasies.

"Put that down," Max barked, "before you kill me by mistake."

"I-is he…?" Eyes wide, she looked at O'Hare's body sprawled on the elevator floor.

"Yes." Max bent, got a hand under each of the guard's armpits, and dragged him out of the elevator. "Did you call Loren?"

"Uh-huh. On his way." Her voice held a frantic note he'd never heard before.

Max straightened. "Did Loren have any idea what happened to whoever was supposed to be on duty?"

"I, uh, didn't think to ask. Sorry, sir."

Max took a closer look at Audrey. She was shaking, and her eyes had a wild cast. He moved to her side, took one of her arms and guided her to a nearby chair. She fell into it. "Take a few deep breaths, dear." He held out a hand. "Give me the pistol. Where do you keep it?"

"Bottom drawer of my desk."

He walked behind her desk. The drawer stood open. He engaged the safety, stuffed the pistol behind a stack of paperwork and a few pots of makeup, and closed the drawer. "Where'd you get that?" She didn't answer, so he pulled up a chair next to her. "I'm not going to turn you in. I was just curious."

She shook her head as if to clear it. More strands of red-blonde hair fell out of her bun and curled around her face, softening her austere features. She'd be quite the head-turner if she let it hang loose. "My brother gave it to me when I got this job. He said I might need it."

"He's a cop, right?"

"How'd you know?"

"Simple. Law enforcement are the only ones authorized to carry those. Nice gun, by the way. Do you know how to use it?"

She opened her mouth to answer, but the elevator door slammed open. Loren, flanked by three hatchet-faced men, rushed into the foyer. "Thank the good Lord you're all right, sir." Loren knelt by O'Hare's side and felt for a neck pulse. "Looks like a clean kill. No blood." He straightened and eyed his boss speculatively. "What'd you do?"

Max shrugged. "I've had martial arts training. I hit him in the neck. Got lucky."

One of the other guards, a solidly build redhead, whistled. "I'll say. That's not an easy blow to get right."

"Get the body out of here," Loren growled. "I've got to figure out where Brady and Hennet are."

Two of the guards grabbed O'Hare, while the redhead punched the elevator button and said, "I'll stay with you, boss, until you can scare up a few more of us."

Max pushed to his feet and held out a hand to Audrey. "Still think you could manage dinner? Or at least a drink to calm you down?"

She nodded and rose unsteadily. "Sure. That would be nice. We need those files. Should've thought to rescue them when you brought O'Hare's body in here."

"Was that what was scattered all over the elevator floor?" Loren asked. When she nodded, he said, "I'll help you gather them up and drive you to wherever you're eating. Once I get a couple of guys to watch over you, I'll come back here and see where my two men are."

"Sounds like a plan." Max jabbed his chin toward the elevator. "After you."

The elevator doors opened. The guards, with O'Hare suspended between them, started forward. Loren held up a hand. "Wait until I get these papers together," he told his men. "No point in getting any more footprints on them."

Max eyed the guards and the dead man. "How about if you haul him out via the roof. You could use a hovercraft, and there'd be less chance of anyone seeing anything."

"Good idea," Loren said. "I should've thought of it. I'll radio for a craft."

"You got it, sir." The redhead jockeyed the stairwell door open and helped the other guards maneuver O'Hare through it, before moving back to Max's side.

"I'd like to get my secretary out of here. She's not used to dead bodies." Max gave a snort of a laugh. "Neither am I, actually. This whole thing's been deucedly unsettling."

"Sorry," Loren murmured, straightening with his arms full of file folders and loose sheets. He shook his head. "Damn if I know which of these went with what—"

"I do," Audrey cut in. "I'll take care of them."

"You can do that later," Max said. "For now, let's just get out of here." He picked up O'Hare's gun and handed it to Loren and then hustled Audrey into the elevator.

~

Loren double parked the electric car outside the restaurant and shadowed them inside, along with the redheaded guard. "Looks pretty good." Loren eyed the private, sound-shielded room. "I'll be right outside, and John will be here too, just as soon as he takes care of the car."

"Once reinforcements arrive, feel free to go hunt for your men," Max said. "You must be worried about them."

"Thanks, boss. I am. Go sit down. I'll scare up a waiter to at least get you a bottle of wine or something. John's going off-shift in an hour, so there will be two new guards outside when you're done eating."

"Thanks for letting me know." Max pulled the door shut and walked to the table. Audrey had already seated herself and was sorting through the stack of papers, arranging them into piles. "It's all right if you don't work for a few minutes," he said, taking a seat across from her.

"It's better if I have something to, uh, take my mind off what happened. You asked if I'd gotten a chance to practice with the gun. The answer is yes. My brother sort of smuggled me into the cop shop gun range in the middle of the night a couple of times. But I've never been around anybody who was dead." Her voice cracked, and she swallowed hard.

Max's estimation of her edged up a few notches. Audrey was one tough cookie, even though she might not realize it. Most women would've dissolved into hysterics.

"You did fine. Good thinking to be in front of the elevator door with your gun."

"Really?" She met his gaze with lovely hazel eyes that were shading toward green and rested her chin on an upraised hand. "I wasn't certain what to do. I thought I should call the elevator back, but I didn't want to subvert whatever you were doing. Then I wondered if I should take the stairs to a lower floor, but that wouldn't have helped if you were still in the elevator… Ach." She rolled her eyes. "Don't mind me. I'm babbling."

"You did fine," he repeated just as the door opened, and a waiter swooped in with a silver bucket holding a wine bottle and two glasses.

"Good evening, sir and madam." The waiter bowed slightly. He was in his fifties with a bald head and merry blue eyes. "The gentleman outside thought you could do with a spot of something relaxing. How does a cabernet strike you? If you'd rather have something different, I haven't opened it yet."

"I'm sure it will be fine." Max held out a hand for the bottle and inspected the label. "What's on the menu tonight?"

The waiter rattled off a series of dishes while he opened the wine. Max glanced at Audrey. "What sounds good to you?"

She smiled warmly. "I'm used to whatever my ration coupons will buy. If it's not too expensive, I'd love to have a steak."

"How would madam like it cooked?" the waiter inquired, arching a brow. He poured a jot of wine into a glass and handed it to Max.

"Rare."

"Salad and rice or potatoes?"

"Salad and potatoes, please."

"I'll have the same," Max cut in and took a sip of what was a very good wine. Rich and oaky, it held an enticing bouquet. "The wine is perfect," he told the waiter, who immediately poured some into a glass for Audrey and added more to Max's.

"This is really quite wonderful," Audrey said once the waiter left. "Everything. Not just the wine. I can't remember the last time I ate out at anything but one of those diners where I flash my wrist computer at the glass cases, and it debits credits from my account."

"Enjoy it." Max smiled. "You deserve to be pampered after what happened. I can still barely believe…" His voice trailed off. He needed to be careful not to say too much. "Um, what's in those documents that's so important?"

She leaned toward him. Her scent was even more intoxicating

than the wine. He caught himself inhaling deeply and pulled away, aware of pressure against his trousers where he was suddenly hard.

Audrey wriggled in her seat. She bit her lower lip and blew out a tense breath. Finally, she lowered her voice and murmured, "I probably shouldn't do this, but I need to be honest with you. It's all in my employment records anyway, but since I was here long before you were governor, well, you may not have looked at them... Cripes! I'm blathering like an idiot. And that's the second time since we got here. Sorry."

"Whatever it is, just go ahead and tell me." Max felt oddly protective toward her, though he didn't understand quite why. Worse, the moment his cock swelled to attention, his wolf had begun a steady patter of lewd side remarks that made Max want to throttle him.

"There's no easy way to do this," she went on, her knuckles so white against the wineglass, Max hoped it wouldn't shatter from the pressure. "If you decide I can't work for you afterward, well..." She set down the stemware and spread her hands in front of her. "Not much I can do about it. I have shifter blood. Roughly 35 percent. Some of my relatives have been killed in this purge, so I'm not the most ardent supporter of the governmental edicts to round up shifters and imprison them."

She sucked in a ragged breath and raised her gaze so she looked right at him. A combination of defiance and pleading etched fine lines around her eyes.

"Miss Westen. Audrey. I'm not going to fire you. It's all right. Thank you for trusting me." Deep inside, Max felt the wolf push him to say more, to tell her about the serum. To offer it up, for God's sake. He resisted. "You told me that for a reason. I assume it's related to the documents. Could you walk me through what's in them?"

She nodded. "Sure. It's intel about something called the shifter underground." Her eyes flashed. "Frankly, now that I know about them, I'm on their side, but don't worry, I wouldn't ever say that publicly."

Max listened as she relayed the story he'd lived for the past couple of days. Everything was there, including the serum that pushed cops with a low percentage of shifter blood into full-blown shifters.

Max was unutterably excited by the prospect of thousands of new shifters to swell their ranks and perhaps turn the tide of the war in their favor. But he smothered his enthusiasm. Hopefully Audrey, bent over the papers balanced in her lap, hadn't noticed his expression change.

Another set of nationwide reports detailed those same cops betraying their oaths and going rogue. Predictions about anarchy ran wild. By the time Audrey was finished, Max was ecstatic, but he couldn't let it show. Everything he'd assumed would happen was playing itself out like a well-oiled machine. He couldn't wait to let the underground know.

"Well?" Audrey looked up from the stack of papers and gathered them together.

"Interesting material. I understand why it was classified top secret." Max tried for a neutral expression. Just because she'd confided in him was no reason to let his guard down.

The door to their private dining room opened. The waiter pushed a cart laden with wonderful smelling dishes. Max's mouth watered. He hadn't eaten since breakfast, and it was pushing nine at night. For the moment, his sexual hunger receded, and he tucked into a succulent, barely cooked piece of meat.

"Where do they get this?" she asked, cutting into her steak and chewing slowly. "None of the shops where I exchange my ration coupons ever have anything but ground or processed meat products."

"There's a black market," he replied around a mouthful of salad.

Her brows drew together. "So it's real," she muttered. "I never paid much attention." Her mouth curved into a smile. She set down her fork and knife. "It's so good, I feel like I should save what's left and take it home. I've already eaten far more than I usually do."

"I can ask the waiter to box it up for you."

"That would be wonderful. Thank you." She glanced at him shyly through long, dusky lashes. "You've taken the worst day of my life and turned it into something special."

He wanted to move to her side of the table and gather her into his arms. Not only was Audrey one of the most stunning women he'd ever seen, she was level-headed and seemingly oblivious to how gorgeous she was. Max put himself on a tight leash. He had bigger problems to attend to than his non-existent love life. At least so far, Audrey hadn't asked about O'Hare's accusations in the elevator.

Christ! Maybe she thought he was tossing the shifter epithet at her.

Max nodded to himself. It made sense. Likely, that was why she'd fessed up about her shifter blood.

"Penny for your thoughts, boss?" She focused her alluring gaze on him. In the low light, her eyes held a violet cast.

"Nothing. Are you about ready to head home?"

She nodded. "I suppose we should. Tomorrow morning will come around early."

He laughed. "Right you are, Miss Westen. It always does. It's all right with me if you take a few hours off—"

She waved him to silence. "Nothing happening at home. The neighborhood's gone to hell. I can't even go out for a walk anymore. All I do is sit barricaded behind a bunch of deadbolts."

Part of him wanted to bring her home with him, to his uptown mansion where she'd have gated grounds to roam. He cleared his throat before something untoward slipped out. "Let me find the waiter." He realized he was still hard and pulled his jacket around to shield the evidence as best he could.

As if the waiter had been waiting right outside and could read his mind, the door opened before Max had gotten up. "Would sir and madam like anything else? A touch of dessert perhaps?"

"You can box up the rest of the lady's meal," Max said. "You wouldn't happen to have that delectable chocolate mousse?"

The waiter's mouth formed an apologetic moue. "Not tonight, sir. We have lemon cheesecake, a cheese and fruit plate with brandy, or ice cream."

"Does any of that sound good?" Max glanced at Audrey. Her eyes were wide with delight.

"Oooooh, it all sounds wonderful. I can't even remember the last time I had real ice cream. That frozen crap they sell nowadays doesn't even have any dairy products in it."

"Could you bring us a sampler plate with a little of everything?" Max asked.

"Of course. Coming right up." The waiter snatched their plates and left.

"Not that I wouldn't love something sweet," she said a bit wistfully, "but I thought we'd decided it was late and—"

Max kicked himself. They *had* decided that—sort of. He was enjoying himself, and he didn't want the evening to end, but that wasn't the sort of thing he could—or should—say to his secretary. He shrugged. "You seem to finally be relaxing. After what happened at the office, you deserve a little R and R. You really can come in an hour or two later tomorrow."

Her gaze softened. "Thank you."

Dessert and brandy were over far too soon. Since he couldn't come up with any more credible reasons to extend their time together, Max followed her out the door of their private dining room. Two security guards flanked it. Max recognized both of them.

"Car's right out front, sir," one said.

"Yes, the waiter kept us apprised of your supper progress," the other added. Tall, lean, and dark, with hard eyes, he and the other guard could've been clones. Max wondered if they were related.

"Whoops!" Max flipped around. "Got to get all those documents. Hold the door, would you?"

"Sorry, sir," Audrey said, looking chagrined. "I should've remembered—"

"No worries, I've got them. They're fodder for the shredder at this point."

They walked out of the restaurant with one guard in front and one behind. Max tucked the ragged document stack under one arm, held the limousine's rear door, and helped Audrey in. "Drop me at the Capitol, and then take Miss Westen home, please."

"I have a car in the garage," she protested, as the limousine rolled away from the curb. "I got here there early enough this morning to park next to a plug, so my battery should be as fully charged as it ever gets."

"Yes, but it's late. I'll send a car for you in the morning. That way I can make certain you've gotten a full night's rest."

"Thank you, sir," she said a bit stiffly. "You've done far too much for me tonight as it is. I don't need to be mollycoddled."

"Is that what I'm doing?" He smiled and turned away so she wouldn't notice. He was treating her more like a date than his employee, but he couldn't seem to do a damned thing to alter it. He aimed for a light, bantering tone. "Here I thought I was just making sure I'd have wide-awake help tomorrow."

"Thank you again, sir." Audrey gazed at her hands. She fidgeted, opened her mouth, and then closed it.

Max started to ask what she wanted to say, but the car rolled to a stop. One of the guards said, "I'll escort you upstairs, sir, and stay until you're ready to quit for the night. I can call in another guard if you'd be more comfortable, or we can grit it out until Bart," he tapped the other guard's arm, "gets back."

"I'm sure we'll be fine for however long it takes him to drive Miss Westen home and return," Max murmured. He didn't want to leave Audrey's warm eyes or her enticing scent. It didn't help that his wolf, nearly mad with lust, was so close to the surface claws pressed against the ends of his fingertips and toes.

Max inclined his head toward her. "Good night. Thanks for the dinner idea. It was a good one." Because he couldn't stop himself, he patted her hands folded in her lap.

The guard who'd spoken got out and opened the limo's back door on Max's side. Audrey glanced away from the sudden glare of the car's dome light. "Who should I call in the morning when I'm ready to come to work?"

Max gathered up the files and documents sitting between them on the seat. Possessiveness raced through him, searing his nerve endings. "Me," he all but growled. "Call me."

Yes. I take care of my own.

CHAPTER 3

*A*udrey leaned against the plush leather seat. Her head spun from far more than wine and brandy. She'd actually just spent several hours with her boss, a man she'd lusted after ever since he was elected as the state's governor a year and a half ago. Even before he'd won the election, she'd been unaccountably excited, viewing his image on the vid feed. What a gorgeous guy, with his white-blond hair and piercing blue eyes. His face looked as if he had Asiatic blood with high, defined cheekbones and a strong jaw. Perfect teeth gleamed when he smiled, which wasn't often. And if all that weren't enough, he was tall, broad shouldered, and wore his tailored clothes like a model.

Shit! I'm even in love with his hands.

She pictured Max's long, tapering fingers and wondered, for the umpteenth time, how they'd feel on her naked flesh.

"Where to, Miss Westen?" The guard's voice shook her out of her reverie.

"I don't live far from here. Midtown. Go to Alhambra and then…" By the time she was done giving the guard directions, a whopping dose of reality had set in. She'd scarcely been a scintillating conversationalist during her time with Max. At first, she'd been so shaken by the phony guard and being right up next to someone dead, she'd been tongue-tied. Then she'd decided she had to confide in him, which was both risky and stupid. A man like him would never consider dating a woman with tainted blood, even if she didn't work for him.

I couldn't date him and not tell him.

Rein it in, sweetie. Last time I checked, he wasn't asking me out. He's a nice man, but not for me.

She thought about O'Hare and the venom in his voice when he'd called her a shifter and a dirty, fucking traitor. She got the shifter part, but the traitor epithet was a mystery. Audrey blew out a sad breath. Ever since the governmental directive targeting shifters, she'd been trapped in a no-man's land where many of her fully human friends and acquaintances shunned her. Oh, they were polite enough about it, but they found excuses to not drop by or accept her invitations to catch a bite or window shop on the vid feed.

Audrey unclenched fists that had balled in her lap. She wanted to be a shifter. She'd had wolf dreams ever since she was a young teenager. From conversations with full-blood relatives, she was certain the striking black and gray timber wolf that stalked her night hours was her wolf. Audrey longed to find out. Though it wasn't sexual, the intensity of her need was akin to what she might feel for a lover. Some nights, it seemed as if she got close enough to breathe her bond animal's hot, wolfy breath… But she always woke empty handed.

"This is the street, right?"

"Huh? Sorry, I need to be more attentive." She glanced outside. "Yes. One more block. It's the multicolored Victorian on the right that's been split into an eight-plex."

"This isn't the best neighborhood. Lots of crime reports originate from these few blocks."

"How do you know that?"

Bart shrugged. "Used to work for the Sacramento City Police Department. Jumped ship about six months ago. They wanted me to take an intravenous infusion. I hate needles, so I looked for another job."

Audrey opened her mouth to ask if he had shifter blood but clacked it shut. People didn't talk about things like that casually. She rubbed her right forearm. It still ached from her first infusion. She'd lied to Max. Far from being ignorant about the black market, she frequented it for things she couldn't get elsewhere—which was just about everything. And she'd known about the transformative serum before reading about it in her stack of intel.

Bart pulled into a red zone, got out, and held her door open. "I'm walking you to your door," he announced gruffly.

"There's really no need. You can watch me from here."

"What floor's your place on?"

"Second."

"I'm going with you. I'll lock the car. It will be fine for five minutes."

She considered arguing but decided it wasn't worth it.

Bart trooped up two long flights of stairs right behind her. The Victorian's lower floor had fifteen-foot ceilings. She clicked keys on her wrist computer to unlock the half dozen electronic deadbolts and pushed the door open. "Thanks and good night."

"Uh, Audrey, I mean, Miss Westen."

Something about his tone bothered her enough to make her muscles tense. She turned to face him. "What?"

"You're a good looking woman. If you'd like to, um, go somewhere just let me know. I couldn't afford anything as grand as where you were tonight, but—"

She laid a hand on his arm. "Aw, that's really sweet, Bart. I don't date. Just got out of a truly miserable marriage, and I need some breathing room."

His tanned skin developed a rosy hint. "Well, offer's open. Just let me know. Be sure to lock up. I'll stand here until I hear every one of those locks engage."

She closed the door and reversed the procedure with her wrist computer to secure it. Apparently Bart was satisfied because she heard his heavy tread fade as he moved toward the stairwell. Audrey glanced around her modest, one-bedroom flat. A couch sat against one wall. Two overstuffed chairs against another had a small table between them. Shelves overflowed with books, an archaic indulgence. A small dinette was just off the even smaller kitchen. All she had was a microwave and a fridge. No one had real stoves anymore, which made food preparation a challenge. The meals she remembered concocting in her mother's kitchen were truly a thing of the past.

I'd never be able to find the ingredients anyway... Or not very often at black market prices.

A screen filled most of one wall. It blinked with messages. She kicked off her high heels, took a seat in front of her computer console, and used the voice module to bring it out of sleep mode. Other than work messages, there was one from her brother. He was the only one she'd confided in about her experiment with the infusions. He was worried about her but couched his inquiry in bland language that could mean anything.

She reassured him she was fine and then drew her sleeve up her arm. A bruise extended from wrist to elbow, but it seemed a little less colorful than it had been the day before when she'd gotten the shot. She planned to wait another day or two and then try to reach for her wolf form. If it didn't work, she'd get another infusion. They were expensive. Five thousand credits. Her brother had told her the cops were getting either five or six. She hoped she wouldn't need that many.

"Doesn't matter," she murmured. "I got a nice settlement with the divorce." She'd taken a lump sum in lieu of spousal support because she didn't trust her ex and figured it would be a battle to get money out of him every month. Audrey commanded her computer to return to sleep mode and pushed out of her chair. She really was tired. It was an hour past when she usually went to bed.

She deactivated the alarm on her wrist computer as she walked to the small bedroom. A bed and dresser took up nearly all the available floor space. Max had suggested she come in late. He must've meant it because he said it twice. She stripped off her jacket and shirt, grimacing as she looked at them. The shirt, which had been crisp and pressed that morning, was a mass of wrinkles. She'd need to launder it. She could try to steam out the suit coat's creases. If that didn't work, she'd need to run it through the building's washer with dry cleaning solvent.

Audrey grabbed hangars from her closet, hung the jacket, and shimmied out of her skirt. She clipped it into place beneath the jacket, started to hunt for her steamer, and decided she'd do it later. She liked to take care of her clothes as soon as she took them off. They lasted longer that way, but it wasn't usually this late when she got home. She stepped into the adjoining bathroom to brush her teeth, take the rest of her hair down, and brush it out. When she caught a glimpse of herself in the mirror, she rolled her eyes. Half her hair had fallen out of its clips, giving her a disheveled look. She removed the remaining clips and pins and picked up her brush.

Yup. A few more reasons he'd never be interested in me. Clothes are a mass of wrinkles. Stockings have runs in them, and I look like I lost my hairbrush.

She returned to the bedroom and ran her hand over the master panel to kill the lights. It left the computer in low power status but didn't turn it off, so messages would continue to flow in during the night. Grappling amid the covers at the end of the bed, she separated the old T-shirt she used for a nightgown from the bedclothes, and got out of her underwear before pulling it over her head.

The soft cotton settled around her. She luxuriated in the feel of it next to her bare skin. The shirt had been another black market item. No one made cotton garments anymore. Everything was synthetic. The cotton fields had long since been swapped out to grow food. Audrey stretched out and snugged the coverlet around her. She closed her eyes, not surprised to see Max's image. Raising her fingers to her lips, she blew him a kiss and then felt like a fool. Tomorrow, they'd be back to business as usual. No more cozy dinners with him close enough to touch.

She inhaled deeply. Even though it was impossible, she thought she could still smell his heady, exotic scent. He smelled like bay rum, musk, and something she didn't have a name for. She'd almost asked him what aftershave he used a dozen times, but the question seemed much too personal. Besides, it wasn't any of her business, though she could've pretended she wanted to buy the same thing for a mythical boyfriend.

She wondered why Max wasn't married. Insofar as the Capitol gossip mavens knew, he never had been. He'd been an international businessman before running for governor. She pressed her tongue against her teeth. She'd tried to dig up background information on Max but ran into enough dead ends to understand he'd had pros erase all but a carefully constructed snapshot of his past. Maybe he was gay. That would certainly explain his lack of female companionship, but he didn't seem to have boyfriends, either, although he might be gun shy of coming out. Worried it might hurt his chances at reelection.

Her eyes widened. Reelection. If he didn't win next time, she'd never see him again. She sat up in bed, suddenly not all that sleepy. Not working side-by-side with Max and seeing him most days was unacceptable. Maybe she could offer to follow him to his next job, whatever it might be. After all, men in charge of things always needed assistants, and he was used to her, a rather large plus in the business world.

"Calm down," she muttered and rearranged herself in bed. "It's two-and-a-half years away. A lot can happen in that amount of time."

Yeah, like he could take up with that columnist who practically lives at the office.

Well, he hasn't yet, so why would he?

Audrey laughed. She was so tired, she was holding nonsensical conversations with herself. What she needed was sleep. Her wolf would be there tonight like she always was. Definitely something to look forward to.

~

SNAPS AND SNARLS dragged her out of a deep sleep.

What the fuck? It sounds like a rabid dog.

Heart in her throat, Audrey reached for the panel that controlled the lights, but her hand wouldn't cooperate. Her body tangled in the sheets, and she struggled to free herself. Surely, if she got a bit closer, she could turn on the lights.

Please God, let the intruder wait that long...

"Calm down. No one else is here. Just us."

"What?" Her panic escalated. *"Who said that?"* The sound of fabric tearing as a sheet gave way was louder than it should have been. What the hell was wrong with her ears? She'd just said something, but she hadn't heard the words. Not out loud anyway. They'd echoed in the recesses of her mind.

"I said it. I'm your wolf. Except you're inside me this time instead of the other way around."

Her writhing body fell off the bed and landed with a solid *thunk* on the floor. *"W-what did you say?"* Audrey lay where she'd fallen, breath knocked out of her.

"Breathe. You shifted. It's not a big deal. Enjoy me. I've waited a long time for you."

Her eyes felt hot and gritty. Her vision was odd, her hearing so acute, she was sure she could hear a faint breeze rustling the tree outside her closed window. She focused her eyes and realized she could actually see.

"Of course you can. Our eyes are much sharper in this form."

So keyed up, breathing was a struggle, Audrey got to her feet—all four of them. She shook out each leg experimentally and then walked around her bed.

"Go ahead. Live dangerously. Let's stroll through the living room."

She snorted. It came out like a low, whuffling rumble. Her wolf had a sense of humor. She made a tentative transit of her flat and then sat on her haunches, marveling at what felt like a miracle.

"How can I be human again?"

"Hmm... Maybe the same way you got to be a wolf?"

"But I don't know what that was. I was asleep."

"Good thing I wasn't. I visit you when you dream, looking for a way in. Tonight, something was different. You accepted me, and here we are." The wolf sounded terribly pleased.

"I'm going to try a few things. I need to learn to move from wolf to human and back again."

"Agreed. Tell me how I can help."

Audrey tried visualizing her human body. She relaxed into it. When that didn't work, she tried to force her way in. After half an hour, she was panting. *"Aw shit,"* she moaned—it came out as a whine. *"What am I going to do?"*

"You're going to keep experimenting until you've got it. I've never heard of a shifter who got stuck in one form or another. You'll figure this out. I have faith in you."

Warmth and tenderness filled her. The last time anyone told her they believed in her was so long ago, she couldn't remember which of her parents had said it. They'd gone into hiding, so she hadn't seen either of them in the past two years. *"Thanks."*

"Think of something that makes you very happy or very sad."

"Why?"

"Strong emotions can help you shift."

Audrey brought up a mental picture of Max. She imagined herself lost in his arms, his mouth pressed hungrily on hers. The wolf woofed approvingly. She deepened her fantasy and imagined herself naked in his embrace. Her nipples pebbled against his well-muscled chest. His cock pressed against the juncture between her thigh and belly, hot and heavy with need.

"*Perfect,*" her wolf crowed. "*You're back. By the way, I like him. Let's find him and fuck him.*"

"*I wish we could. It's more complicated than that.*"

"*Why? Sex is never complicated.*"

Audrey shifted from foot to foot and realized there were only two of them. She felt her way to the bedside table and drew a black market candle and matches from its single drawer. She lit the candle with quivering hands and sank onto the edge of the bed. "Shit!" she muttered. "I can't believe it. The infusion worked. I'm really and truly a shifter. Finally."

She thought she should jump up and down and whoop her delight, but her body trembled from head to toe. Probably an overabundance of adrenaline from all her attempts to shift back into it.

"*No,*" the wolf said sagely. "*You're shaky because you want that hunky man so much. Let's go find him and—*"

"*Is this one of the sideline benefits of being a shifter? You maintain a running commentary in my head?*"

"*Yes. Do you have a problem with that?*"

Audrey thought about it. "*No. Not really. It will take some getting used to, though.*"

"*I think you should shift again. It gets easier.*"

"*How would you know?*"

"*I just do.*"

She took a measured breath. Her wolf was right. She did need to practice. If she didn't get more of a feel for the transformation, she might shift spontaneously at an inopportune moment. "*All right.*"

Audrey visualized the wolf—no, her wolf, she corrected herself —in all her lupine glory. This time, she felt the transformation. Her body lengthened; her limbs moved beneath it.

That wasn't so bad.

She trotted from room to room and then visualized her human form. This time simply thinking of herself as human worked without ginning up a sexual fantasy about Max. Encouraged, she pushed herself though two more cycles.

Human again, she blew out the candle and lay on her shredded sheets. She supposed her T-shirt was somewhere in the wreckage.

No matter, I can get another one. Since I don't need any more infusions, I won't have to watch my pennies quite so closely.

"I'm going to sleep for a little longer," she told her wolf.

"Fine. I'll watch over us."

A glow started deep in Audrey's belly. The partner she'd dreamed of for years was finally in her head and by her side. It took some of the sting out of knowing she could never be with Max. Her thirty-five percent shifter blood would've been a hard sell, but now that she could shift, human men were definitely off limits. With a surge of feral protectiveness, she knew she'd do whatever it took to keep herself and her wolf out of harm's way.

CHAPTER 4

*M*ax drove back to his uptown mansion around one in the morning. He hadn't been terribly efficient working through things, or he'd have been home a couple hours earlier. No matter how hard he tried to concentrate, all he could see was Audrey. The dimple she got in her cheek when she smiled. The sparkle in her eyes when she was intrigued by something. Her masses of honey-colored hair with its reddish cast... His groin tightened. He forced himself to focus on bringing the car to a stop. Crashing into the wrought iron gates was not a good idea.

He clicked buttons on his wrist computer, and the gates to his estate swung open. He waited until the car behind him carrying both security guards cleared the gate before closing it. He'd invited them to wait out the night inside his house, but they'd demurred.

"We need to patrol outside," Bart had told him. "Not much good for us to hole up in your cozy kitchen. We wouldn't hear a bad guy until he was on top of us."

Max considered arguing that his house staff person provided more than adequate protection, but he still felt guilty about giving Loren and his boys the slip the previous night.

I'll behave myself. Maybe that will give me a little latitude the next time I need to go check on the underground. Speaking of which...

Max drove the hundred yards to his Tudor-style mansion set toward the back of a half-acre lot. Flood lights flared, bathing the front of the house in light. He gathered his briefcase, stuffed to the gunnels with intel he'd perused earlier, and trotted up broad flagstone steps to huge, carved double doors. His fingers hovered over his wrist computer to retract the locks, but the door slid open.

"Sir. You're late tonight." Johannes was clad in jeans that rode low on his hips. His chest was bare and his shoulder length, dark brown hair sleep-tousled. The muted alarm, which sounded in the house whenever the gates opened, had probably wakened him. Head of security for the shifter underground, Johannes was a mountain cat shifter and one of Max's oldest friends.

Max's capital security team thought Johannes was his butler and manservant, who provided personal protection as a sideline. At least so far, no one had questioned Max's choice of household staff.

"Feel like a cup of coffee in the upstairs study?" Max quirked a brow.

"Of course, sir. Coming right up." Johannes peered through the door at the car pulling up behind Max's. "Who are they, and will they be joining us for coffee?"

Max shook his head. "They're guards from the Capitol. It's a long story. I'll explain once we're settled." Johannes would understand what Max meant. He wanted them in the secure portion of the house where they'd be safe from electronic surveillance.

Fifteen minutes later, Max had traded his tailored dark blue suit for silk pajama bottoms and a well-worn, cotton three-quarter robe. Both were teal, one of his favorite colors, although he couldn't wear it to work since it wasn't professional enough. He strolled into the walnut paneled study with metal embedded in every wall. Johannes was already there. He'd slipped an old fisherman-knit sweater over his bare torso. His green eyes were pinched with worry.

The minute the door closed, he said, "There you are. If you'd taken much longer, I would've gone looking for you."

"Humph. Guess you weren't really asleep."

Johannes rolled his eyes. "Of course not, but I saw two cars come through the gates and had no idea who was with you. Playing dumb can work to one's advantage." He slammed a fist down on his thigh. "How could I have been asleep? The attempt on your life was all over tonight's vid feed. I've fielded fifty calls from the underground headquarters. The only thing I did just now, besides make coffee, was call Ryan to reassure them you're okay. What the fuck happened?"

Max chuckled. "It's good to be needed—I suppose." His smile faded. "It's possible my identity's been compromised. The assassin named me as a shifter just before I killed him. Get Ryan on the secure channel."

Lithe as the cat he was, Johannes sprang to his feet, brought the wall screen to life, and clicked keys on his wrist computer.

Ryan's face appeared. At six-feet-four, he was a bit taller than Johannes, with hair red as flame and hazel eyes. His forehead scrunched into anxious lines. "Boss. Thank Christ! We've all been huddled around the vid feed for hours. All they'd say is someone with a long criminal history tried to kill you, and that the man is dead."

"He's dead all right. I killed him. Ryan, you've got to find out who else knows about me. I have no idea how much O'Hare—if that's even his real name—actually knew. He was masquerading as one of the guards. I hate to admit it, but he damn near got me and my secretary into the garage. I'm sure there was a car with accomplices just waiting to take me down. Anyway, I figured out something wasn't right and reversed the elevator. Once he knew the gig was up, he called me a shifter and a dirty, fucking traitor. He was definitely set to kill me—"

"How'd you know he wasn't a guard?" Johannes broke in. "It's damn lucky you saw through him."

"My wolf smelled him."

"Ah, credit for my good deeds." The wolf preened.

"Be sure to thank him for us," Ryan murmured.

"I already did." Max bit back a grin. No matter how grim things got, his wolf always made him feel better.

"Do you think it's safe for you to go back to the office until I'm done digging around?" Ryan asked.

"Solid point. Probably best if you work from here for a while," Johannes said.

Max shook his head. "No. I can't let them know they've rattled me. It's got to be business as usual."

Johannes took a slug of coffee. He poured another cup and handed it to Max. "How about if I put my fancy duds on and go to work with you?"

Max swallowed some coffee and considered it. "Well, Loren—"

"Who's that?" Ryan cut in.

"Head of the security team at the Capitol."

"Now that you mention it, I just might know him. Go on."

Max leveled a glance at both men. "No more interruptions until I at least get a complete sentence out. Now, as I was saying, Loren knows I have internal security personnel. Given what happened earlier tonight, it wouldn't seem odd if I brought one of my own men along. How's your false identity du jour, Johannes?"

"Bulletproof." The shifter grinned. He'd been in international espionage in one capacity or another since before Napoleon's time.

"Great." Ryan blew out an audible sigh. "It's settled. I'm going to sign off and get to work. Devon will help. He has great intel connections all through California. Of course he's laying low right now, but he can tell me who to contact. I'll let you know as soon as I find anything, no matter how trivial. Um, boss…"

"Uh-huh."

"If I come across something that doesn't sit right, we're hauling you in. We need you heading up the underground way more than California needs a governor. They've got redundancy in the House and Senate. No one like you, of course..." Ryan's gaunt cheeks turned crimson.

It was Max's turn to blow out a tense breath. "That will be a last resort. And it has to be my call. Understood?"

The muscles rippled in Ryan's jaw. "I understand, but I don't totally agree. You're more of an optimist than me. Also more of a risk-taker."

"It's why we're a good team. Report as soon as you know something."

The screen faded to gray. Max drank half the cup of cooling coffee before setting it down. He turned toward Johannes. "That's all for tonight. Try to get some sleep. We're due in at seven, which is —" he glanced at his watch "—less than five hours from now."

"I'll have something made for breakfast by six." Johannes strode toward the door.

"Thanks. Don't know what I'd do without you."

Johannes's face split into a broad smile; it turned his austere features into something quite attractive. "That makes two of us."

Max stared at the leaded glass panes over his teak desk and finished his coffee. Muted lights flickered in crystal sconces. Floor to ceiling bookshelves held a selection of literature dating back to the sixteen hundreds. His study was a cozy retreat with its solid wood furniture and leather upholstered easy chairs. He'd recreated something very similar in dozens of houses over the long years of his life.

He steepled his fingers and rested his chin on them, thinking he should be more worried about whatever might be unfolding in some subterranean corner of the universe. Anyone who'd figured out his true identity was a force to be reckoned with. Normally, he'd have pulled out all the stops to identify and eradicate anyone and everyone who knew about his dual life.

I am doing that. I sicced Ryan on them.

Yes, but I should've joined him. All I'm doing is mooning over Audrey. The real reason I don't want to work from here is I wouldn't see her.

"I told you—" his wolf cut into his thoughts *"—we need to finish what we started tonight. She's ripe for the plucking that one."* A randy howl made Max laugh.

"Aren't you worried? Someone just tried to kill us."

"You don't seem to be, so why should I?"

Max got to his feet. The wolf had a good point. He walked down the hall to his bedroom suite. It took up about half the third floor. Johannes had commandeered the entire floor above.

Once inside, he touched a panel and one wall came to life with the Caucasus Mountains. Max never tired of looking at them. He'd been born there during a time when he and other shifters were valued for their magic. The computer program had several choices for a living wall mural, but Max always chose this one. It had been far too long since he'd left the States. Maybe this would be a good time to plan a vacation. He hadn't had one since taking office as the state's governor.

He wondered what Audrey would think about western Russia and then mentally shook himself.

She works for me. I can't proposition her—about anything. If she went on a trip with me, she'd never be able to come back and work for me. The gossip crew would have a heyday, and they'd make her life a living hell. Even if we were circumspect, someone would find out. They always do.

He kicked off his slippers, lay on the large, raised bed, and let his mind drift. He wasn't surprised when he found himself engaged in a replay of his hours with Audrey. He twisted his head from side to side, stretching out his neck and trying to dissolve the iron bar of tension sitting just between his shoulders. Max felt confused, an alien emotion. He prided himself on his analytic skill and the crystal clarity with which he viewed the world. He'd worked with Audrey for a year and a half. Sure, he'd noticed how attractive she was, but what in particular had happened today to plant her front and center on his radar screen?

Max puzzled through what was different. He wasn't any lonelier than usual. He'd come to accept his unattached status. Much to his wolf's chagrin, sex, for the sake of release, lost its allure long ago. He remembered Kate Roman saying something like that, but she'd taken a different path. She hadn't given up on sex. Until she met Devon, she'd made a living working as a sex surrogate. But she had given up on finding a shifter mate, just like most of them did, he supposed. It was rare to find your mated one. The only reason they hadn't died out entirely was they'd taken to breeding with humans. Of course, it produced diluted blood, but so long as a child was at least fifty percent, they'd still be able to bond with their animal and shift.

His mind wandered to the mating ceremony he'd performed for Kate and Devon after breakfast at the safe house just that morning. They'd looked so happy, and they'd positively reeked of satisfied sex. Max wished them well, yet jealousy stabbed. They had what every shifter wanted—the special one destined to bond with them throughout time. There was a second part to the mating ceremony that had yet to come. He'd watch them couple in their mountain lion form. While they were joined, he'd mark them with the mating stone a second time.

Max snorted. He couldn't believe the mating ceremony had been less than twenty-four hours ago. It seemed he'd lived through several lifetimes since then. He was glad his wolf wasn't nattering about finding them a shifter mate. It didn't help matters. Max wanted a mate, but it wasn't as if he could go to the vid feed or a store and select one. Shifters being under a death sentence didn't help. Most potential mates were probably in deep hiding. With his wolf's help, he could sniff out who had shifter blood, but knew better than to bring the topic up publicly. He'd been shocked when Audrey spilled the secret about her mixed blood at dinner. No one ever talked about things like that.

Audrey.

As if thinking about her drew her near, her scent, all honey and musk, rose out of his memory and enveloped him. His cock twitched. In seconds, it curved against his belly, as hard as it ever got. Before he was even aware what he was doing, his hand snugged around his shaft. He wanted to come. Needed to. Wouldn't be able to sleep without release.

Since when do I need an excuse to jack off?

Max stroked his erection. He closed his eyes and imagined Audrey's tawny skin and multi-colored eyes. All that glorious hair fell to her waist. Peeking out from behind its thick curtain were generous breasts. In his mind, he licked and tongued them into stiff peaks. Her back arched, and he could almost hear her little, panting moans as she begged him to fuck her, to sink his full length inside her hot wetness. She pressed a hand between their bodies and took hold of him. In his fantasy, it was her hand stroking his hard-on, urging him onward.

He pushed her down onto a softly-carpeted floor. Her arms twined around him, nails digging into his shoulders. About the time he dipped into her glistening mound surrounded by red-blonde curls, his cock jerked in his hand. Hot semen splattered his chest and stomach. The harsh sound of his breathing was loud in his ears. He gulped air; there wasn't enough in the room.

When his heartbeat steadied, he got up and found his way to the bathroom. He glanced at the sunken marble tub and shower with its sunflower head. Both would wake him up. He settled for a warm washcloth and cleaned the evidence of his passion from his body. He was still hard. Max knew he could come again, but he wanted the real thing, goddammit. Not his hand married to his rich imagination.

This time when he laid down, the mountains on the wall opposite the bed comforted him. "If worse comes to worst," he murmured just before he fell asleep, "I can go home. Lots of places to hide myself there for a decade or two. By the time I surface, maybe the world will have changed."

"You're not going to do that. We stand and fight our battles."

Max groaned. *"I need sleep,"* he told the wolf.

"We don't need to run away to Russia. We need Audrey."

Max felt his lips tug into a smile just before darkness closed around him.

~

THE CHIME of his wrist computer dragged him from sleep. It was still dark outside, but he'd set his alarm for five-thirty to give himself time to shower. By the time he stepped out of his bedroom, ready for the day, briefcase in hand, it was a couple of minutes past six. Johannes would have a full breakfast laid out because he also liked eggs and toast and bacon.

Succulent smells intensified as Max worked his way down two flights of stairs to the main floor where the kitchen and dining room were. He pushed the swinging door into the kitchen aside and saw Johannes, back to him, working at the stove. "There's fruit and French toast on the table," he said. "Omelet coming right up."

"You're chipper this morning." Max laid his briefcase on a chair, shrugged out of his suit jacket, and sat at his usual place in the kitchen eating nook. In the grand tradition of country kitchens, this one could've housed a small family. Glass fronted walnut cabinets lined three walls. Stainless steel appliances gleamed in the incandescent light from a Swiss chandelier. Max poured orange juice and dished up fruit, French toast, whipped butter, and raw sugar.

"Not exactly." Johannes set two plates on the table and sat down. "Ryan called me about an hour ago."

Max sucked in a breath, batting back annoyance—and trepidation. "Why didn't you get me?"

Johannes shrugged. "You were still asleep. I thought that was more important. Let me fill you in, and then we can call Ryan. He'll be expecting us."

"Well?" Max set his fork down. Suddenly, he wasn't particularly hungry.

"The short version is the State Attorney General's office is interested in you. They've been tracking you for quite some time now."

Max drew his brows together. "I wonder why."

"Maybe because the AG is as conservative as they come, and you're the most liberal governor California's ever had. Anyway, that's not relevant. Ryan thinks they're looking for criminal activity, or anything they can dig up to discredit you."

"And they found something better than their wildest expectations." Max's jaw tightened.

"Not exactly. Ryan doesn't think—"

"Get him on the vid feed," Max barked. "I need to hear this from him."

The screen mounted between two banks of cabinets flared to life. A grim-faced Ryan appeared moments later. "Morning, boss."

"Spill it."

"What did Johannes—?"

"Never mind. Start at the beginning."

Ryan nodded. "The AG's office has been watching you since before you took office. This last little go-round in Berkeley, where the entire tracker task force for the city police department quit en masse piqued their suspicions, more specifically the suspicions of the investigator assigned to you—"

"Holy, fucking shit. You mean to say that I've had my own personal asshole tracking me the whole time I've been governor?" Max slammed a fist on the table. "He must be damned good. I never knew."

Max turned an ear inward, but his wolf was silent. Maybe he was ashamed someone had gotten that close to them without him realizing it.

"I'll just bet the Berkeley mess got their attention," Max went on. "The city hired those guys to track down shifters and kill them. To have most of the task force turn into shifters because of a serum the brass forced on them, and then to have them defect right along with the human members of the force, must've come as quite a shock."

"It was long overdue," Johannes muttered. "We've needed a break ever since they amped up their efforts to wipe us off the face of the earth."

"Anyway," Ryan went on, "we took care of *your own personal asshole*. He had shifter blood, so we shanghaied him and gave him a whopping dose of the serum, enough to force him into a shift. You can bet he'll lay low from here on in." Ryan made a sound between a snort and a grunt. "In case you're interested, he's a bear. I really like his bond animal. Hopefully, the investigator will grow enough to be worthy of the partnership."

"Brilliant." Johannes clapped his hands together. "A trained spook. Have we offered him work?"

"Not yet. He needs to stop cursing me first. We've got him locked up. We won't let him out until we're certain he won't betray us."

"When will that be?" Johannes asked.

"It shouldn't take long. He understands he has to learn to control his newfound abilities. Once he does, he'll come to appreciate them. There are advantages to being a shifter—lots of them. He's a smart man. He'll come around."

Max drained his juice. "What's our next move?"

"We're in the process of infiltrating the investigator's records and destroying them. By the time another person gets around to recreating them—if that even happens—your term should be close to up."

"I love it." Max stuffed a bite of omelet into his mouth. "Sow confusion. Make them afraid. The next fellow might not be so quick to raise his hand and volunteer if he thinks he might end up either dead or compromised."

"I'm not sure about dead or compromised." Ryan pursed his lips. "The best case scenario would be if we can send the investigator— Connor Bastion—back to his desk. He'd be a real asset in an undercover capacity."

"Sounds like a plan." Max nodded approvingly and continued working on his breakfast.

"There's more," Ryan said. "The phony security guard who tried to kill you was a friend of Bastion's. O'Hare was in the military, but they discharged him for mental instability. We're not totally positive, but we think the assassination attempt was him acting on his own. Connor seemed as shocked and upset about it as we were."

Max started to breathe a bit easier. Maybe this wasn't as bad as he'd feared. "Hook him up to the full body lie detector."

"Devon's already on it. In the meantime—" Ryan's sharp gaze skewered both of them "—be damned careful. Max, watch your back. And, Johannes—"

"Yeah?"

"Do not leave Max to even go to the john."

"Fine. I'll piss in the wastebasket."

"That won't be necessary." Max stifled an eye roll. "My office suite includes a bathroom."

"If there's nothing else—" Ryan nodded curtly "—I want to sit in on Devon's session with Connor. Sometimes those electronic readouts are a bitch to interpret."

"Go ahead. We'll be in touch."

Max watched the screen gray out and then glanced at the time. "We need to leave."

"Car's out front. I alerted the security men they'd be shadowing two of us to your office."

CHAPTER 5

Max scrolled through documents that needed his e-signature. He'd been working for the better part of three hours, ever since eight, when his early meeting about the pathetic condition of California's highways had ended. Scarcely a day went by when they weren't sued by a citizen who'd been injured because of gaping potholes or missing road signs.

Most meetings were empty rhetoric. Frequently, the only thing accomplished was determining a date for the next get-together. This morning's conference hadn't been any different. Several legislators had issued press releases regarding their intent to fix the problem, by God. They'd taken up most of the hour reading them to the group. Max's ears still rang from a boatload of sincere-sounding drivel, with fists pounding the polished oak table for emphasis.

Johannes stifled a yawn from where he sat sprawled in a corner. "How do you stand this? It's incredibly boring."

"You're supposed to be alert. Vigilant. Maybe you should stand near the door like a real guard." Max lowered his voice to a whisper. Johannes's feline hearing would pick it up. "You know why I took this job. I never meant for it to be permanent. Politics disgust me. It's basically one side cutting deals with the other in a back room.

No one cares about the electorate. Politicians want to keep those special interest donations rolling in. They have a pretty sweet life, and they'll do damn near anything to hang onto it."

Johannes stood and wandered to the door. "I can hear everything on the other side without standing right next to it," he grumbled.

Max frowned and shook his head, shooting a meaningful glance at his friend. "You only think you can."

Johannes winced, obviously realizing his error in case anyone had been monitoring their conversation. "Of course. You've caught me dead to rights, sir."

Max turned his attention back to the vid feed screen. Johannes didn't spend much time in public. He needed to take care not to reveal he could hear and see things beyond the ken of human senses. Max's wrist computer vibrated. He glanced at it. Joy whooshed through him. Worse, his cock leapt to attention. Audrey was ready to come to work. He texted that he'd send a car immediately.

Stop it! He told himself. *When she gets here, I need to look like her boss, not a besotted adolescent.*

His fingers hovered over the computer to call the Capitol security team and ask them to get Audrey, but then he had a better idea. "We've been at this for a few hours." He grinned at Johannes. "Let's take a break. We can swing by, pick up my secretary, and get something for an early lunch while we're out."

Johannes angled his head to one side, regarding Max through narrowed eyes. "You sound awfully excited about something you could send one of your many underlings to do."

"Do I?" Max aimed for neutrality.

"You forget. I've known you for a very long time. Sure. Let's go. I'm looking forward to meeting whoever's got you all hot and bothered."

Max stood and moved to the coatrack to get his jacket. "I am not—"

Johannes hissed in a stage whisper, "You can't fool me. Remember, I can smell…things."

Max shrugged into his suit coat. He did not want the conversation to go any further where someone might hear. He dragged his jacket over his erection and buttoned it. Of course Johannes would be able to smell arousal.

"After you, sir." Like a proper manservant turned bodyguard, Johannes held the office door open.

"Thank you." Max inclined his head.

Loren and another guard Max didn't recognize snapped to attention. "Where are you going, boss?" Loren asked. Max peered at him; the man looked exhausted. Riding on intuition, he glanced at Johannes. "Get the car from the garage. I'll meet you out front."

"Where are you going?" Loren asked again. "We should go with—"

Max crooked a finger and stepped back into his office. Loren followed him and closed the door, understanding Max wanted privacy. "Did you find your men?" Max asked without preamble.

Loren's eyes turned to ice chips. "Yes. Dead."

Max laid a hand on his arm. "I'm sorry."

"Thank you, sir. One of them was my son-in-law. Daughter's pretty busted up."

Max exhaled slowly. "If there's anything I can do—"

"Appreciate the thought. Brady knew what he was getting into when he went to the police academy. So did Hennet. Way things seem to be heading, it will be a miracle if any of us survive. When that governmental directive about shifters was codified, I was grateful I was less than 50 percent."

Max tried to keep quiet, but the words slipped out. "Why did you tell me that?"

"Because now I wish I had access to shifter magic. Hell, I'd take any edge I could lay my hands on. Murdering human scum have the run of the streets." His blue eyes held a haunted edge. "Sorry, boss.

No reason to lay my worries on your doorstep. Hell, they tried to kill you yesterday."

"Tried is the operative term. I'm still here."

Loren stood ramrod straight. "Now, about your destination with your bodyguard—"

"If it makes you feel better, you can trail us with a car. We're just going to pick up Audrey and get something to eat. She was pretty shaken by what happened yesterday. I told her to take as much of today off as she needed and to call me when she was ready to come to work."

Loren's eyes softened. "She's a good woman. Almost like a daughter to me. I worked with both her father and her brother at the Sacramento County Sheriff's Office. Her brother and I are still friends." Loren leaned closer and spoke low. "Father disappeared right after the shifter edict came down. I figure he went into hiding. Damned shame. He was a fine officer."

"Do you know where he is?" Max pitched his voice equally low.

"Why?" Loren's voice vibrated with suspicion. He moved back a few steps as if worried he'd said too much.

"Not the reason you're thinking." Max creased his forehead in concern. "If you're right about the streets being overrun with criminals, it struck me that if Audrey's father, uh, disappeared, others like him did also. We could use every trained man, that's all. We can't afford to have them moldering away in bunkers or wherever they've gone to ground."

"I couldn't agree more, boss, but if they come out of hiding—"

"I know. It's a big, fat, fucking problem. Let me give it some thought. The other states are in the same boat we are..." Max let his voice trail off before he revealed more than was prudent. "I need to run. I don't want Audrey standing out in front of her house for any longer than she has to."

"Why the hell didn't you tell her to wait inside?"

"I did. She said her place is in the back, and she can't see the street. She doesn't know I'll be getting her. She probably thinks I sent you or one of your boys. Anyway, we'll talk more later." Max tugged the door open and trotted through it, intent on riding the elevator to ground level. By the time he got there, Johannes stood next to the open passenger door, waiting.

"The security guy told me they're tailing us." Johannes jerked his chin toward a car sitting right behind them in the *Load and Unload Only* zone.

"They are." Max slid into the car. "Come on. Get in. That way, we'll be ready to roll as soon as Loren, or whoever he sends, shows up. I'll sit in the front seat. It will be easier to talk that way."

Johannes got behind the wheel and shut the door. "Do they do everything in pairs?"

"Mostly. Why?"

"When I started in this business, we preferred to work alone. Less chance of being compromised."

"That was over three hundred years ago."

Johannes gave a Gaelic shrug. "Things haven't changed that much. Too many people knowing anything always spells trouble."

"We're picking up a woman and lunch. It doesn't matter who knows."

"It always matters, my friend." Johannes glanced in the rearview mirror. "Looks like we're good to go here. Do you have an address?" Max rattled it off and then entered it into the onboard nav system. The fully electronic car would find the house without any assistance from Johannes.

Max swallowed a grimace. He knew Audrey's address because he'd looked up her personnel records the previous evening and then felt like he was trespassing. By the time he'd pried his eyes from the screen, there wasn't much he didn't know about Audrey Westen. Born and raised in Bend, Oregon, she was the second of two children born to a seventy-five percent shifter father and a human mother. The family had relocated to the Sacramento area when she was ten. She'd finished high school with honors and gotten a degree in business from UCSF. After that, she'd gone to work for the

California State Legislature and moved from there to the Governor's office. She was twenty-nine years old and had been married once for five years. The final divorce papers were issued eight months ago. She had no children.

"Are you going to tell me about her?" Johannes asked, his voice so soft Max wasn't certain he'd even heard the question except subliminally.

"She's—uh, no. No, I'm not."

"Why?" Johannes glanced sidelong at him and grinned. "You never know, I might like her too. It's been a while since we shared a woman."

Max's wolf reared up, close to the surface. Savage possessiveness knifed through him. "This one isn't for sharing," he gritted through clenched teeth.

"Maybe not. She works for you, so doesn't that mean you can't fuck her at all?" Another Gaelic hand gesture. "These modern rules. There are so many of them, I can't keep track."

"You're absolutely correct. Staff is off limits."

"Who made that rule?"

"Funny," the wolf sniped. *"If I recall, I asked the same question."*

Frustration soured Max's stomach. He balled his hands into fists. "Leave me alone. Both of you."

"Who's the other—? Never mind. Must be your wolf."

Max snarled, realized they were slowing, and knew they had to be close to her house. "I'll join her in the backseat once we pick her up."

Johannes laughed. "I'll try my damnedest to behave."

"That would be a first. On a different topic, Loren, head of Capitol security, just told me he's sorry he's not a shifter."

Johannes quirked a brow. "Interesting. Does he have shifter blood?" Max nodded. "I'll have Ryan run a background on him. Are you thinking we could make him an offer?"

"Exactly. Depending on what you find out. It would be handy to have inside help as I continue to infiltrate the government's structure."

"You're playing a dangerous game, old friend."

"Tell me about it."

"Someday shifters will put your face on coins."

Max snickered at Johannes's attempt at dry humor. "Let's hope I live that long. Besides, you missed something. No more coins. Just credits. Even the black market only deals in bills. Easier and cleaner to round totals up or down."

~

AUDREY PACED from one side of her living room to the other. She glanced at her wrist computer again. Another couple minutes and she'd move to the curb in front of her multiplex. She smoothed nervous hands down the front of her black skirt and checked her jacket one more time in the mirror. A teal silk blouse was tucked into the skirt. Its fabric felt delightful next to her skin. Silk garments weren't available anymore, either, but no one controlled what she bought at the black market.

She bit her lower lip, feeling conflicted. After getting a few hours' sleep, she'd gone on the vid feed and made discreet inquiries based on the intel she'd studied the day before. She was nearly certain she could find the shifter underground enclave in Hayward —or get damned close. She'd hatched a plan over coffee as the sun came up and done a few things to set it in motion. Like withdrawing credits and trading them for black market cash at a twenty-four hour pawn shop three blocks away. She had a little time. If she built her cash supply slowly over a couple of weeks, it was unlikely anyone would notice.

She squared her shoulders. If she went through with her plan, her life was about to change in ways she'd never be able to reverse.

Yeah, it's not as if I get a do over on this one if things don't work out.

She'd typed a letter of resignation, e-signed it, and sent it to her in-basket at work. Once there, she'd take it to Max.

Audrey shook her head. That was the hard part. Max. She'd never see him again, and it scored her soul down to its very roots with bitter acid. "It's not as if he'd want me, anyway. Other than maybe to bed and forget." She spoke aloud to steady her resolve. Not that she wouldn't love a roll in the hay with Max, but she had more important obligations than being a slave to her libido.

The shifter underground needed help. They'd reached a pivotal point where it looked as if they might develop enough momentum to stage an effective counterattack. Maybe, if they were successful and the governmental edict was repealed, she could return to Sacramento and see if Max might be interested…

Too many maybes. Besides, I'd still be a shifter, and he's not.

But Dad married Mom. He was a shifter, and she wasn't…

Audrey quashed the ray of hope. It would just divert her and might pose a threat to her resolve.

"I still say we should find him and give him a run for his money," her wolf murmured. *"He's one fine looking man from the image in your mind last night."*

Audrey rolled her eyes, grabbed her briefcase, and walked out the door. It didn't help that her wolf, while the most wonderful creature ever, loved sex. She trotted down the steps, pushed the main building door open, and stopped dead.

Not Loren. Max.

He stood outside the car, holding one of its rear doors open. As always, he was impeccably dressed in a tailored dark suit, white shirt, and abstract-patterned tie. His blond hair gleamed in the midday sun. He grinned, and her heart did odd things.

"Boss. I expected—"

"Yes, yes." He held out a hand to help her into the car. "I've been at the office since seven. Needed a break, so I rustled up Johannes—that's who's in the driver's seat—and we headed your way. Not to worry, Loren's team is here too." He gestured toward a car idling behind them.

Audrey got in and arranged her skirt. Suddenly, she wished it were just a little longer. Her throat tightened when Max walked around the rear of the car and slid in next to her. She wondered if she'd be capable of talking if he asked her something. His intoxicating scent filled the car. It set her nerve endings on fire. Her nipples hardened, and all the moisture in her body headed south. Mouth dry, thighs slick with arousal, she bit back a moan.

What the fuck is wrong with me? I've never had to hold myself back from jumping a guy's bones.

"Hi there. I'm Johannes." The man in front half turned and looked appraisingly at her with eyes that probably didn't miss much. "Max has told me so much about you—"

"You said you were going to behave," Max cut in.

"The mademoiselle is truly charming." Johannes was still gazing at her.

She tugged at her skirt again. "Nice to meet you. I'm Audrey." She nodded in his direction without exactly looking right at him. Her cheeks were warm, and she knew she was blushing.

"I thought we'd grab a bite as long as we're out and about," Max said, smiling at her with a ten-thousand watt grin that made her want to throw herself into his arms.

"Uh, sure. Fine."

"Any preferences?"

You mean like stripping off all our clothes and—

She pressed her thighs together to quell the fire raging through her nether regions and shook her head. "Whatever you feel like is fine."

"Are you all right?"

His voice was full of compassion. It nearly undid her. *Focus,* her inner voice hissed. *Remember my decision.* "Yes. Thank you for asking. I'm just tired."

"Are you sure you feel up to working today? You really could take the whole day off."

She couldn't meet his sea-blue eyes. If she did, all bets were off. "It's only half a day at this point, boss. I'll be fine. Really. Besides, I need to rescue my car." She looked out the window. Anywhere but right at him.

How am I ever going to be strong enough to march into his office and tell him I quit?

More to the point, will I even make it through lunch without embarrassing myself?

CHAPTER 6

*M*ax settled against the butter-soft leather seat. He'd shrugged out of his suit jacket before getting into the car. He needed something to fold over his lap to hide his erection. The front of his trousers belled out. No way to mistake what was under them. He swallowed hard and tried for control. When he'd seen Audrey waltz out of her building and down her steps, it took every shred of willpower at his disposal not to race to her and sweep her into an ardent embrace.

He wanted to pull her hair out of its clips and pins and run his fingers through it. He needed to close his mouth over hers and taste her, craved feeling her breasts pushed against his chest.

Holy Christ! I've got to stop this. I'll come in my pants.

What's wrong with me? This is way worse than it was last night.

"Sir." Johannes's tone carried a sharpish edge.

Max focused with difficulty. "Yes?"

"I've asked you twice. Where are we going for lunch?"

His brain felt muddled. "Maybe that fish place. It's between here and the office."

"Excellent choice." Johannes fiddled with the onboard computer.

The car moved forward. "I'll let the rest of the security team know our destination." He tapped his wrist computer and held a hurried conversation.

Max wove his fingers together under his jacket to keep himself from reaching out and touching Audrey. She was inches away. If his nose were a judge, she was just as aroused as he. The musk of her sexual heat made it almost impossible to think. He turned toward her. "Did you sleep well?"

"In fits and starts. You?"

"About the same."

"Why are you making small talk?" His wolf sounded outraged.

"To be polite."

"You can be polite later. She's our mated one. Do something before I do it for you. Remember the first mating always involves me."

Max sat straighter. His wolf couldn't possibly be correct. Audrey wasn't a shifter—well, not one with enough blood to shift. Thirty-five percent wouldn't do it. Some fifty percenters couldn't even shift. His mated one had to be a shifter, just like him.

"We'll talk about this later."

"I want to talk about it now."

Sharp points of claws pressed against all his digits. If Max weren't vigilant, the wolf would force himself out. *"I'm having a hard enough time. Leave this alone for now."*

A deep, snarling growl reverberated in his belly. The wolf was retreating, but probably not for long.

"Did something just happen?" Audrey looked away as soon as he raised his gaze.

"Not really. Guess I'm more tired than I thought. Why do you ask?"

She shook her head. "Not sure. For a moment there, you looked a bit, uh, rattled. Not as composed as you always are."

The car slowed, and Johannes pulled into a loading zone. "How about if you get out here? I'll find a better parking place and join you inside."

"Sure." Max got out with his jacket draped over an arm held close to his body and moved to Audrey's side of the car. She didn't wait for him, though, and was already standing on the sidewalk before he got anywhere close to her door.

The car with Loren's men stopped inches away. One of the guards got out. "I'll take over until the other guys figure out where to leave the cars." He let out a grunt. "Downtown parking. I swear. It gets worse every day. Don't know how places like this stay open. It's not safe for patrons if they have to walk several blocks to anywhere."

A hovercraft flew low overhead. The guard cursed and radioed something from his wrist computer, probably on the police scanner channel.

"They're not allowed inside the city limits, are they?" Audrey asked.

"No. Air quality's at stake. It's not their electric engines, but the onboard generators that do damage." Because he wasn't thinking, Max took her arm. A pleasure-laden shock traveled from his fingers directly to his groin. Thinking the relative dimness inside would be welcome, he tugged gently. "Come on. Let's see if they have a table for us."

She leaned into him so close it was hard to breathe. "Even if they don't have one, I'll bet they make one for you."

Max bit down on a reply. He'd never been comfortable with having people fall all over themselves to serve him. That was one part he definitely wouldn't miss when he left the governor's office behind. He led her into the establishment and was greeted by an enthusiastic maître d'. The rotund man with short, graying hair led them down a hallway and into a spacious dining room. There were only about ten other customers. "Would that be a table for two, sir?"

"Three." Max kicked himself for not telling Johannes to wait with the car.

"Actually, five." The security guard hurried to their side.

"How about this?" Max pressed a twenty in black market cash

into the maître d's hand. "Put the lady and I at one table and the other three men at a table close enough they feel they can protect me but not so close they hear every word I say."

"I understand." The maître d's gray eyes glittered mischievously.

Johannes and the other guard strode briskly into the restaurant. "Where are we sitting?" Johannes asked.

Loren's man looked down his nose. "The boss and his lady are dining privately."

"She's my secretary, not my lady," Max corrected sharply. "We'll be discussing work. Don't worry, you'll be close enough to lay down your lives for me if anything happens."

Johannes shot him a knowing look and took each of the other men by an arm. "Where are the three of us?"

"Right over here, sir." The maître d' bustled them to a table near the center of the room. When he returned, he ushered Max and Audrey to a window seat overlooking a small, gated garden. "Will this do?" he inquired archly.

"It's lovely." Audrey sat without waiting for either man to pull out a chair for her.

"Yes, it will be fine. Do we have menus today?"

"No, sir. We're serving salmon. You can have it cold in a salad, or warm with turnips and new potatoes. The soup is bouillabaisse. It's also available as an entree with fresh bread."

"Can I get the salmon salad and bread?" Audrey asked.

"Of course. And for you, sir?"

"I'll have the bouillabaisse. A bottle of something white like a Chardonnay would go well, I think."

After the maître d' left, Audrey frowned. "Booze in the middle of the day? I really will fall asleep at my desk."

He shrugged. "I spent a lot of time in Europe. They have large lunches and take off part of the afternoon to sleep."

"Yes, but don't they work until nine or ten at night then?"

He smiled. "I'm surprised you know that."

"It's a small world, courtesy of the vid feed." She glanced up, her eyes alight with interest just like they'd been the night before. "Seems like we have the worst of both worlds. We don't get the elaborate lunches, or the naps, and we end up working till all hours, anyway."

He laughed. She had such a bright, inquisitive mind, and her analysis was spot on.

"Don't laugh at me." She laid her purse in an adjacent chair.

"I'm not. I was thinking how astute you are, and it tickled me."

She leaned toward him. "I know it's not proper, since I work for you and all. But if you could lay that aside for a few minutes and tell me about yourself, I'd love to listen. Who's Maximillian Sigayev?"

It wasn't proper. Beyond that, it had been a very long time since he'd shared much about himself with anyone, but to his surprise, Max opened his mouth and started talking. He used the carefully constructed background he'd developed for himself, but still, her interest blasted through his defenses and touched him in a place he kept under lock and key.

SOMEWHERE BETWEEN HER initial shock at being face-to-face with Max and struggling to manage her arousal, Audrey decided to let the lunch play out as it would. There'd be plenty of time once they were back in the office for her to tell Max she was resigning. Her wolf had kept up a running tirade about mated something-or-others. Audrey hadn't completely understood what her bond animal meant. Thank God, the wolf finally subsided once Audrey stopped fighting her attraction toward Max. A little shocked at how quickly she'd rationalized away a few hours of indulgence, she was mildly ashamed of herself, but she pushed the discomfort aside.

Because it seemed like the only opportunity she was likely to get, she asked Max to tell her about himself, never expecting he would.

Guess today is one for miracles.

She listened as the man who haunted her dreams with nearly as much frequency as her wolf, talked about growing up in Maine.

"I was an only child. My parents were older, and I think I was a bit of a surprise. We lived in the hinterlands north of Bangor, maybe fifty miles from Mount Katahdin. I spent my boyhood and adolescence hunting and fishing. Never liked school much, but I did all right. Went to Boston College and graduated in Economics. Dad and one of my uncles ran an international import business, so I went into the family business. I lived in Russia, Spain, and Italy for a few years each, but I missed the U.S. Came back here about three and a half years before I decided to run for governor."

Audrey listened carefully. She was pretty sure she was in love with Max, so she wanted to know everything about him. Something didn't quite add up, though. His story was almost too practiced, as if he'd memorized a script.

"I tell you, he's our mated one." Her wolf was back with bells on. *"That means he's a shifter. He's much older than that cock-and-bull story he just spewed."*

"Be quiet. I can't think when you're in my head."

"I'm afraid you'll let him get away. You don't understand how critical this is. Our mates don't grow on trees. We're damned lucky if they show up at all."

"Audrey?" He raised an inquisitive brow. "Earth to Audrey. Goodness, I'm telling you what you wanted to know, and it feels like you're a million miles away."

"Here we go." A black-coated waiter sashayed to their table carrying a tray stacked with food. He arranged the dishes in front of them with skill and flair. "I'll be back in a moment with the wine."

"I'm sorry." She met Max's gaze and felt like she was drowning in the incredible deep blue of his eyes. "I was listening. Really." She glanced at the food and unfolded her napkin in her lap. Everything looked expertly prepared and smelled delectable.

She took a bite of her salmon salad. "How do the restaurants manage? This has to be—" she lowered her voice "—black market food."

He buttered some bread, dunked it in the fish chowder, and ate it. When he was done swallowing, he said, "Much of it is."

"Why don't the authorities do something?"

Max snorted. "Because then they wouldn't have anywhere to eat."

She felt naïve. Despite working at the state Capitol, the universe of privilege and special deals that benefited the wealthy, but no one else, was a world she knew very little about. The wine arrived. They ate in a companionable silence for a few moments.

Johannes walked to their table and pulled out one of the extra chairs. He smiled but looked tense. "There is a back way out of here," he said very softly. "Exit the dining room, turn right, and go to the end of the hall. The car will be waiting for you."

Audrey opened her mouth to ask what had gone wrong. Her heart thudded heavily in her chest. Fear made it difficult to take another mouthful. Max met her gaze and shook his head very slightly. "Thanks for stopping by," he said brightly, aiming his words at Johannes.

"No problem, sir. Always a pleasure to see you." Johannes rose and walked out of the restaurant with a deliberate pace. Not too fast, not too slow.

"You needed to visit the ladies room?" Max kneed her beneath the table. "It's just down the hall. Think I'll take advantage of the men's at the same time." He rose in a fluid motion, picked up his jacket and got her purse, which he handed to her.

"Yes, of course," she murmured. Her legs shook. Balancing on her high heels as she walked across the room took almost more finesse than she could manage. The other security guards still sat at their table, but they weren't eating. Their eyes were everywhere as they chatted with one another.

Finally, she and Max reached the doorway. She'd been expecting a laser to rip through her any second. Not that the hall was any safer, but at least it was a more manageable space. Once they were heading down it, Max took her arm and picked up the pace. He didn't say a word, but he was so close his breath was hot against the side of her neck as he shielded her body with his.

"Governor, what a surprise." A masculine voice boomed from the far end of the hall, back toward the dining room.

Max bent close and spoke right into her ear. "Keep going. Do not stop until you're in the car with Johannes. He'll take good care of you." He gave her a pat on the ass and turned. "Senator. Thought I recognized your voice."

Audrey kept moving. She was too keyed-up to listen in on Max's conversation with one of the legislators. It had actually sounded like Senator Bellotti. Then the door was there and she pushed through it, ignoring the alarm that blared when it opened. The car was, indeed, waiting. She yanked the passenger door open and jumped inside.

"Where's Max?"

"Someone he knows from the Capitol stopped him."

"Goddammit." Johannes slammed a fist into the steering wheel. He tapped furiously into his wrist computer and then spoke into it, "Keep a sharp eye. Do not let anything happen to him. I'll be back as soon as I can."

The car lurched away from the restaurant's back door and down a narrow alleyway. "Where are you taking me?" she asked.

"Good question. Where would you like to be taken?"

"I think Max expects me to be at work."

"I suppose it's as safe as anywhere. Certainly a better choice than your house." He blew out a terse-sounding breath.

"What happened back there? Why'd you tell us we had to leave?"

"I can't give you particulars, mademoiselle, but you were in danger."

Her heart seized. It was a full time job to keep her wolf at bay. "Is the bad guy still in there?"

"I'm afraid so."

She clutched Johannes's arm. "Turn the car around. We have to go back for Max."

"He's our mated one. We cannot leave him. Jump out of the car. Run back. Now."

Audrey's fingers curved into claws. One emerged, dark and shining, and snagged on Johannes's jacket sleeve. She yanked her hands into her lap and fought the transformation with every shred of her being.

"Stop that," she told her wolf. *"If people find out, we're screwed."*

Johannes glanced at her partially transformed hands with an odd expression on his face. "Get hold of yourself. Take a few deep breaths. Max has two guards to watch over him. Besides, he's a big boy. He's pretty competent taking care of himself."

The claw retracted, and she inhaled shakily. Why hadn't Johannes said anything about seeing it? Desperate to change the subject, she asked, "How long have you known him?"

"Long enough."

"I think it's more than that. There's something easy between you that makes me think you grew up together or something."

"We didn't."

"Man of few words, eh?"

"Not always. I would lay down my life to protect Max, though. You'd be wise not to forget that."

"I'm fond of him myself." Her eyes widened. "Ah crap, I can't believe I just said that. Forget you heard it, okay? Must be the wine."

Johannes chuckled. "No worries, mademoiselle. I suspect Max is *fond* of you as well. There's no easy way to say this, but you must learn to keep your, ah, other side under better wraps. This is your building. I will drop you within sight of the uniformed guard next to the front door. When you get out, run directly up the steps and go inside."

"Where are you going?"

"Back to help Max."

"I thought you said he didn't need any help."

"He doesn't, but I feel better when I'm close enough to do some good. Out, mademoiselle."

She opened her door. "Don't let anything happen to him." The pleading in her tone stunned her.

"I don't plan to. Close the fucking door, so I can get out of here."

$\mathcal{M}$ax walked slowly until he heard the back door open and shut. Christ! Everyone in the place probably heard it. The alarm went off like a klaxon. He quickened his pace. "Senator Bellotti. What a nice surprise." Max extended a hand.

The plump, middle-aged Italian grasped it with a sweaty palm. With a knowing smirk on his face, the senator glanced down the hall. "What did you do to that poor girl? She was so anxious to get away, she went through a fire exit."

"She's just racing home to warm the bed for me. You know how they are."

"Well, I used to. Not quite as, ahem, active as I was when I was just a young blade like you. Say, I wanted to bend your ear about that mess in Berkeley yesterday."

Max nodded. It made sense. That was Bellotti's district. "I think everything's more-or-less under control—" he began.

The senator rolled his eyes. "Not judging by the volume of messages bombarding my office. What can we do to reassure people they aren't going to be ripped to shreds in the streets by shifters who've run amok?"

Max sat on anger that flared, pushing it deep so nothing would show on his face. He tried for a placating diversion. "Normally, I'd say time would cure things, but we're close to the end of our resources. Water's a huge problem in the southern part of the state. We're going to have to tighten the ration coupon system, and people always react badly to that."

"What does that have to do with my people's immediate safety?" Senator Bellotti asked indignantly. His dark eyes were nearly lost in folds of fat. Greasy dark hair was plastered against his scalp. Expensive aftershave nearly choked Max's hypersensitive nose.

Max took a measured breath. He wanted to say it was obvious the senator hadn't missed very many meals, so he couldn't fully appreciate the looming ration coupon crisis. Instead, he murmured, "Everything is interconnected. People panic when basics like food and water are threatened. There will be an influx of people leaving southern California. Many of them will land in the Bay Area, straining already thin resources—"

Bellotti waved him to silence. "Never mind. I get all that. What are you going to do today about my problem?"

Sock you in your overfed gut?

Max forced a smile. "How about this. You get together with the four other Bay Area senators. Call my secretary, Audrey Westen, and make an appointment. We can brainstorm some solutions."

"I don't want an appointment next week."

Max swallowed irritation. "You can have one later today if you get moving on it."

Something changed in the air currents. Maybe a different scent made it through the curtain of Bellotti's aftershave, maybe something even more subtle caught his attention. Max threw himself over Bellotti's body and drove both of them to the wooden floorboards.

"What the fuck?" Bellotti's muffed shriek was drowned out by the *phut-phut* of laser weapons.

"Stay down boss," someone, probably one of Loren's men, called. "We're on it."

"Yeah," the other yelled. "Put that tub of lard on top of you."

"I resent that." Bellotti writhed beneath Max's weight.

"Stay put, goddammit," Max hissed. "You'll get us killed." More gunfire. Muted shrieks. Max's wolf lobbied hard, pushing for a shift.

"Let me out. I can get us out of here."

"Yeah, right. Blow our cover all to hell. Shut up. You'll get your turn. Just not now."

"At least you got our mated one to safety."

Max didn't reply. His wolf seemed so certain about Audrey, but Max wasn't buying it. His mated one would be a shifter—just like him. Audrey was an amazing woman, but she'd find another human partner, not a shifter like him. Pain hit him just beneath the solar plexus. It was so intense, he wondered if he'd been hit, but then he realized the sting was emotional. The thought of Audrey wrapped in another man's arms drove him mad with jealousy.

"There are lots of shifter-human matings," the wolf said. *"Besides, you're wrong about her. She's just like us."*

"We'll talk about this later. I need to concentrate to get us out of here."

After what seemed like a long time, but was really only minutes, silence descended. "You can get off me now. I'm sick of eating dust. They really should clean this place better," Bellotti complained.

"We stay put until my security squad tells me it's safe to move."

"Who wants to kill you? This is, what, the second attempt on your life in twenty-four hours?"

"How do you know they weren't after you?" Max countered. "After all, you're the one with all those relatives in organized crime."

"Bullshit! You have no right to—"

"Oh, stand down for Christ's sake. Your background's not exactly a state secret. How about thanking me for saving your sorry ass? The lasers would've cut right through both of us. Look." He pointed to gaping holes in the wall inches above their heads.

"I can't see shit. You've got me pinned."

"Okay, you can take my word for it."

Footsteps raced toward them. Arms pulled Max to his feet.

"Boss. Thank the good Lord you hit the deck." The guard, a blond who looked as if he lived at the gym, brushed dust off Max's sleeves.

"Yeah, what tipped you off?" Loren, who'd arrived at some point after Max left the dining room, hurried to Max's side with three other security personnel. "We saw the bastards sneak in through a side door. I knew you'd been warned and figured you'd be safe in your car. Why didn't you leave?"

Max hooked a thumb at Bellotti. "He needed to talk with me."

Red-faced, the senator looked as if he'd run a race, or tried to. He was breathing so hard, Max wondered if he weren't about to have a heart attack or stroke.

"If I'd known what a shit magnet you were," Bellotti muttered, "I would've kept my mouth shut."

Max tapped Loren's arm. "Assign a man to drive the senator back to the Capitol or wherever he wants to go."

"Thanks," Bellotti said dully. "I'll take my own car, but if they could follow me, that would be great."

"Now, about that meeting," Max said.

"Never mind." Bellotti shook his head. "It's not safe to be around you." He stalked down the hall. One of the guards ran after him.

"Come on." Loren tugged on Max's arm. "Let's get you out of here."

Johannes burst into the hall and launched himself at Max, thumping him on the back. "You're looking alive. Sorry I missed the fireworks. Must've been a hell of a show judging from the fissures in the walls."

Max turned to face Johannes. His heart had to be in his face, but hopefully only someone who knew him as well as Johannes would see it. "Audrey?"

Johannes smiled. "She's fine."

Max shut his eyes; relief coursed through him. When he opened them again, he said, "Let's get out of here. Be sure and tell the proprietor we'll take care of any damages."

"I'll handle that part," Johannes said. "But not right now. I'll call him once you're back in your office."

Max walked out of the restaurant flanked by Johannes, Loren, and four other guards. He headed toward Loren's car, but Johannes grabbed his arm. "You might want to drive with me. We need to talk."

"Fine." A muscle in Loren's jaw twitched. "We'll be right behind you. Sure you don't want one of my guys in the car?"

"If you put us in the middle with a car in front and one behind, that's probably a better plan," Johannes suggested. Max heard compulsion running beneath the words. It was part of Johannes's shifter magic.

A corner of Loren's mouth turned down. "Hate to admit it, but I agree with you. See you back at the shop."

Max sat in the front seat, not caring what the rest of the security squad thought of the arrangement. As soon as Johannes shut his door, Max asked. "Bugs?"

"Nope. Swept the car—again."

"What the hell happened? Who's targeting me?"

"We're working on it. Ryan thinks it's one of those virulent anti-shifter groups like *Take Our Country Back* or *Humans Unite.*"

"But no one knows I'm a shifter. Not for certain." Max clamped his teeth together. "Besides, I thought it was the AG's office."

"Vigilante groups have always operated by the same rules: kill first, ask questions later." Johannes took a breath. "The only thing we know about the AG's office is they assigned an operative to you, and O'Hare happened to be a friend of his. Based on the full body lie detector data on our brand new bear shifter, Ryan's convinced the AG's office had nothing to do with O'Hare's attempt on your life."

"Great. So O'Hare belonged to some sort of radical vigilante group. Do I need to go into hiding?"

"Do you really want me to answer that? I'm the one who thought you shouldn't leave the house until we got to the bottom of this. You, on the other hand—"

"Enough. What did you want to talk about?"

"Audrey."

Max's stomach tightened. Johannes had spent time with her. Was his friend about to disclose he wanted her for himself? Or worse, they'd had a skirmish in the car. Audrey had been so hot, it wouldn't have taken much to make her come. Maybe she'd seen an opportunity and taken it. After all, Johannes was a magnificent man. All shifters had an almost ethereal beauty, but he was even more eye-catching than most.

It was hard to articulate his next words, "What about her?"

Johannes grinned. Max's heart sank into his shoes. He recognized that grin: knowing and lewd. He and Johannes had shared enough women over the years.

"Well." It was clear Johannes was enjoying himself and was going to drag this out. "She was quite upset at the prospect of leaving you behind. More than upset—distraught."

Max groaned. "Don't tell me. You comforted her. Damsel in distress and all that."

"Not that I didn't want to, but she got so wound up, the hand she had on my arm turned into a paw."

Max's eyes widened as the implications sank in.

"See," his wolf crowed. *"Told you so. She's just like us."*

"W-what happened then?"

"I told her to get herself under control. She obviously doesn't have very much experience keeping her bond animal hidden. They can be damned headstrong."

"I resent that." The wolf broadcast his commentary, so Johannes would be sure to hear.

Johannes grunted. "Resent all you like. It's the truth. My cat is just as reckless and impulsive. He needs me, whether he knows it or not. Just like you need Max."

"Great." Max slammed a palm against his forehead. "Now you're talking to my wolf."

"He wanted me to hear him." Johannes tossed a hand skyward in one of his trademark gestures.

"Could you tell what kind of paw?"

"Huh?" Johannes scratched the stubble dotting his chin. "Oh, of course you'd want to know. All I saw was a claw and a bit of fur. It could have been anything. Wolf, bear, cat. Who knows?"

Max shook his head, still assimilating the information. "I don't understand. Unless her personnel records are fake. They say her mother was human and her father seventy-five percent shifter. By my count, that pegs her at roughly thirty-seven percent, which isn't enough to shift."

"It is curious." Johannes took over driving from the nav system and maneuvered the car into the underground parking garage. "I could be wrong, but I'm almost certain she hasn't been able to shift for very long. If I hadn't helped anchor her human form with a spot of magic, I think she would've shifted right here in the car."

"Mmph. Arousal could've fueled the transformation." Max's jaw tightened. "Did she, uh, come on to you?" He steeled himself for an answer that would destroy him.

"Strong emotions push us to shift, but I don't think you have much to worry about. She was frantic about your safety. Damn near forced me to turn the car around. I think that's why her bond animal wanted out: to return to you."

"It's a lovely theory, but—"

"It's more than a theory. You didn't see the look on her face." Johannes parked in Max's personal spot right next to the elevator.

Something hot and bright speared Max, catching him in the heart. He pushed the car door open, got his briefcase from the backseat, and loped to the elevator.

Johannes joined him. "You're supposed to wait until I get out of the car and can cover you," he chided.

Max rolled his eyes. "Yes, Dad."

Johannes spun Max to face him and placed a hand on each shoulder. "Goddammit!" he snarled. "This is not a joke."

"Chill out. Let go of me. The elevator's here."

"We can catch the next one." Johannes waited until the door closed. "There have been two attempts on your life. Serious ones. If you weren't what you are, both probably would've been the end of you. We—" he moved a hand and jabbed a finger into Max's chest "—cannot afford to lose you. And I'm not talking about the State of California."

"Lighten up. I'm still here."

"Indeed. We're having a meeting tonight at nine with Ryan, Devon, and our primary folk in Europe and the U.K. We'll make some decisions."

"What if we're not home by then?"

"Arrange things so we are. Ryan and I floated a bunch of times. Nine our time is five in the morning for our partners. It worked for everyone."

"What are you hoping to accomplish?"

The cat shifter switched to telepathic speech. *"The first order of business is finding out who wants to kill you. If we can manage that, it might be safe for you to keep your dual life intact. If not, we need to rethink things."*

"What if I don't agree with the consensus?"

"You know the answer to that." Johannes dropped his hands to his sides.

Max pushed the button to call the elevator. He did know the answer. The shifter hierarchy managed by group decision-making. If they decided it was too risky, they'd ask him to step down from his governorship, except he wouldn't be stepping down, he'd simply disappear. Long before he was declared dead, his lieutenant governor would take over, and then there'd be a special election to replace him.

They rode up in silence. The door whooshed open on a foyer full of people, who wanted to talk with him.

Audrey glanced up from her work and said, "They have numbers. I'll send the first one in as soon as you tell me you're ready."

Max clamped his jaws together, forming a determined line. What he wanted to do was whisk Audrey into his office, gather her close, and make the rest of the world go away while he asked her about what Johannes had seen. Instead, he picked his way through the crowd, smiling and pressing outstretched hands. A few tried to talk with him, but he shook his head. "Later. When your turn comes."

Johannes followed Max up the interior stairwell and into his office. Once inside, he secured the door. Max took a cursory look at his electronic inbox and groaned. "Shit! There's enough work here to keep me busy until tomorrow—and that's without that crowd in reception."

He clicked the display on his wrist computer. "Audrey."

"Sir?"

"Find out what each of those people needs. Group them so I can see several at a shot. I'm ready for the first bunch whenever you send them my way."

"I'm on it, sir."

Hours later, Johannes ushered the last group of legislators and concerned citizens out of the office. Max got to his feet, went into the washroom, and bent to douse his face with cold water. It was just past seven. Maybe this would be a good time to leave. It would give him and Johannes an opportunity to eat something and get home in time for the meeting.

When he came back to his desk, Audrey stood next to it holding a piece of paper in her hand. She looked absolutely beautiful. Not a hair was out of place. She stood a bit stiffly, though. Max wondered what was wrong. "Did we miss someone? It's okay, I can talk with a few more folk."

"No, sir. That's not it." Her eyes glistened as if she were trying not to cry. "It's just—aw hell, there's no easy way to do this. I'm resigning, sir. Effective two weeks from today's date." She laid the piece of paper on his cluttered desk, spun, and walked out of his office, closing the door behind her.

*T*here. *I did it.*

Audrey made her way down the back staircase to her office one floor below. Tears spilled down her face, but it didn't matter. She had everything packed up and sitting on her chair. All she had to do tonight was get out of the building, and then she could cry her eyes out.

"*You can't do this,*" her wolf snarled. "*You have to go back up those stairs and tell him you didn't mean it.*"

"*I'm doing what I have to. I thought you, of all people—or animals or whatever—would understand I'm doing it for us. So we can be free again.*"

"*But he is one of us. Why won't you believe me?*"

"Because it would be too good to be true," she muttered and made a blind grab for her purse, briefcase, and coat. Between her overflowing eyes and inattention, she pitched headlong into Loren standing next to her desk.

"Princess," he murmured, borrowing her father's pet name for her. "What the hell happened?" He drew her against his chest, and she sobbed helplessly, unable to hold onto even a semblance of composure in the face of his kindness.

"I-it's nothing," she managed finally. "Cumulative stress from the past couple of days. I-I can't work here anymore. I just went upstairs and gave notice."

Loren stroked her hair. "I understand. Place has turned into a real pressure cooker."

She turned her tear-streaked face up to look at him. "Do you know where my daddy is?"

His eyes narrowed. A muscle twitched beneath one of them.

"Tell me," she breathed. "Please."

"I can't. I promised him."

"Surely you didn't promise not to tell his children."

"Oh, but I did. What you don't know could make the difference between staying alive—or not."

More tears cascaded down her face. Loss cut deep. First her family and now Max.

I never really had him to lose.

Loren drew her close again. "There, there. Hush. I'll see you home."

She shook her head. "No. I've got to get my car out of the garage. I'm taking up one of the charger spots. They'll fine me." Her voice sounded muffled against his chest. She was probably getting mascara all over his white uniform shirt.

"I'll see they don't."

"What the hell is going on here?" Max burst into the foyer, with Johannes on his heels. He reached for Audrey, but Loren's arms tightened around her. "Let go of her. That's an order," he barked.

"Sir." Loren's gaze sparred with Max's. Audrey lifted her head and watched two sets of blue eyes, both like ice chips. Max looked as if he were ready to do battle for her. Even though she tried to stifle the feeling, his protectiveness thrilled her.

"Audrey is like a daughter to me," Loren went on. "Her father and I used to be...friends. I told you that last night. She's upset. I'll see she gets home."

"It's all right." Audrey levered herself out of Loren's grasp and faced Max. "I'm not sure what it looked like to you, but he was comforting me."

Johannes inserted himself smoothly between Loren and Audrey. "We'll take care of her and see she gets home. I'll text you once she's settled."

"I really can take care of it," Loren insisted. "Audrey, what do you want to do?"

Sink through the floor.

Throw myself into Max's arms and never let go.

Max's blond hair had escaped its customary queue and hung around his face. His blue eyes held a wild note that sang to her soul. He was so exceptional, it was hard to tear her gaze away. She opened her mouth to say she wanted to drive herself home, and Loren could follow her, but what came out was, "It's okay, Loren. Max and Johannes can see me home. I'll text you too, once I'm safe."

"Are you certain?" Loren walked to her side. She nodded. "We never got to finish the part of our conversation about your father," he went on. "Let me know when a good time would be to do that."

"I will. Thanks, Loren." She raised up on tiptoe and kissed his cheek. The older man colored.

"No problem, princess. Glad to have helped." He turned and disappeared through the stairwell door.

"Looks like you're ready to leave." Max eyed the briefcase, coat, and purse still clutched against her body.

"I was on my way out when I ran into Loren." She managed a wan smile and wondered how blotchy her face was from crying. "Guess I sort of lost it. It's been a tough couple of days."

Johannes looked from one to the other. "How do you want to do this, sir?"

MAX GLANCED at his wrist computer. Seven-twenty. What he wanted to do, and what he could do given the war council webcast meeting scheduled for nine, were two very different things. "I'll go with Audrey in her car, so long as it's acceptable to her. You can follow us, and we'll go home from there."

"I'd really be okay driving by myself."

"Not going to happen." Johannes pushed the call button for the elevator. "You look like you've been crying your eyes out. The least we can do is deliver you to your door."

Audrey squared her shoulders and looked at Max. "You can come with me under one condition."

Max quirked a brow. "What might that be?"

"No discussion about my letter of resignation. My decision's final." Her voice shook, and her chin quivered slightly.

"All right. No discussion about that. At least not tonight." A corner of his mouth turned downward. "No promises about tomorrow, though."

A smile ghosted across her wan face. "I'll take what I can get."

The elevator door opened. Max gestured Audrey through. His stomach was tied in burning coils. He wanted her so badly, he could hardly keep his hands to himself. He was painfully erect, and his wolf wouldn't shut up.

"Let me out. Then her wolf will emerge, and we'll get things straight."

"Two wolves in the front seat of a car driving across town is not a good idea."

"Fine, do it after we get to her house."

"How do you know she's a wolf?" Max was curious.

"Instincts. Mine are sharper than yours."

The elevator opened onto a deserted garage. "Wait under the light," Johannes snapped, "while I do a sweep."

"Where's your car?" Max asked.

"A couple of levels down where employees park."

"Johannes, come back here. We'll drive to her vehicle."

Max was careful not to touch her for long when he helped her into the backseat of his car. If his fingers lingered for more than the barest of moments, he wouldn't be able to let go. They rode in silence to her car, an old two-seater. Audrey got out, popped her trunk, and dumped her things inside. She unplugged the car from the wall charger next to it and stowed the cord in the trunk along with her belongings.

"Usually, I keep everything in the passenger seat," she explained, "but that won't work if you drive with me."

Max wanted to divert her attention from her decision to allow him inside her car. He was well aware Johannes's magic had something to do with her capitulation upstairs in the office. "I haven't seen one of these cars in a long time. Where'd you get it?" He held the driver's door open for her and then went around and got into his seat.

"It belonged to my father. He used to like to work on it. Taught my brother auto mechanics on this car."

"Not you?"

She laughed, seemingly feeling a little more at ease, as she engaged the electric motor and punched buttons on the onboard nav system. "Me? A little. I was more of a nature-girl than a get-grease-on-my-fingers one."

Max had intended to keep his distance, but he was so drawn to her, the plan went up like so much fairy dust. "I live in an arboretum. Maybe tomorrow after work you could come home with me and take a look. I keep greenhouses as well as outside plants, so something's always blooming."

He heard her suck in a breath. "Oh, I'd love to… But it's not a good idea."

"Why not?" Max chided himself the minute the words were out. He didn't want her to feel boxed into a corner. "Um, sorry. Shouldn't have asked you that. I respect your decision."

They exited the garage, and Audrey turned the car over to its nav system. She repositioned herself so she could look at him. "No, maybe we do need to talk about it. I'm much too attracted to you for my own good. I'll be leaving the area soon, and it's probably better if we don't spend too much time together." The expression on her face made his heart ache. Bittersweet, resigned, and fatalistic, she looked like an ancient warrior preparing to engage in a hopeless battle but determined to see the thing through to its conclusion.

"I know I promised not to talk about your resignation. And I'm not, not exactly. I understand why you'd want to quit your job, but why do you have to leave Sacramento? If you weren't working for me—" He bit back the next words. She'd obviously been sobbing her heart out in Loren's arms. Not good to overload her with how much he wanted and needed her.

"I have something important I have to do. It's why I quit."

"What? Maybe I could help."

She shook her head. In the muted glow from the car's interior lights, her eyes looked haunted. "You wouldn't want to."

"Try me."

"Look. Could we let this drop please? We're nearly at my house. What we should be talking about is how you want me to structure the time I have left before I leave."

Yes, but that's not what I want to talk about.

While he was working on what to say next, she pulled into a small parking lot adjacent to her building. With a mind of its own, Max's hand covered one of hers. "Audrey." His voice was raspy with denied need.

She turned to face him. Her full lips trembled. He drew her toward him in the small confines of the car and covered her mouth with his. She tasted sweet, like summer wine. Her arms twined around his neck, and she opened her mouth beneath his. Max's heart rate accelerated. He held her as close as he could, given the console between them. The musk of their combined arousal was fragrant in his nose. He could have held her for hours, reveling in her taste and smell.

The lights from Max's car lit the night when Johannes pulled up beside them. Audrey wrenched herself away and opened her door. "I shouldn't have done that. I'm going inside now, and you're getting into your car and going home. If you follow me into my house, we both know what will happen." A catch in her voice contradicted the resolve in her words.

She exited the car and latched her door.

If it weren't for that damned meeting, I'd—

Max unfolded his long legs and got out of the car. He caught up to her. "I'm not sorry, Audrey. You're one of the most beautiful women I've ever known. Not only that, you're bright and inventive and—"

"Stop. All that flattery will go straight to my head, and I might become impossible to be around. See you in the morning...boss." She lengthened her stride and disappeared through a side door.

"Are you going to just stand there all night?" Johannes called.

Max sighed, walked toward his waiting car, and got in. "No, but I'd like to."

"Did you ask her about—?"

"No. Tonight wasn't the time. It's only a ten minute drive from the office to her house, and I knew we needed to hustle home for the meeting you scheduled."

"You'll have more opportunities to talk with her."

"Not all that many. One of the things she told me is she's leaving town."

Johannes's forehead creased as he ferried the car back onto the city streets and told the computer to take them home. "Not sure I like that."

"What do you mean?"

"You won't appreciate this, but hear me out, anyway. It seems she can shift when she shouldn't be able to. And now she's leaving town right after a couple of attempts on your life. Do you suppose she's working for whoever's out to get you?"

"Not possible," Max blustered.

"Oh, but it is. I knew you wouldn't take it well. When you're a little calmer and not so aroused, you can roll it around in your head."

"If she's working with any of the shifter groups, they want me alive."

"Not all of them. Some blame you and the underground for the increased surveillance and those elite tracker task forces that have been rounding us up and killing us. This is a relatively new development and one of the things we'll be talking about tonight."

Max inhaled and blew the breath out sharply. Audrey couldn't be working for the enemy. She just couldn't. He turned an ear inward, expecting to hear a protest, but his wolf was silent.

~

Audrey barricaded herself behind her phalanx of deadbolts. Her heart was light, her body delightfully provoked. She could still feel the pressure of Max's mouth on hers. Her lips tingled from the aftermath of their kiss.

Maybe we could make love once before I have to leave.

"Yes. Call him. Get that other shifter to turn the car around and leave Max here."

Audrey laughed as she pulled pins and clips from her hair. It cascaded around her body. *"You're incorrigible."*

"No. I just know what I want. We need him. He's our soul mate. Our mated one."

Audrey moved into the bedroom and got out of her clothes. After washing her face and brushing her teeth, she snugged a soft, synthetic robe around herself and brought the vid feed to life, intent on continuing the research she'd begun the previous night. After she'd gotten credits ready to transition to black market cash tomorrow and checked a few more sources for the location of the underground's headquarters in Berkeley, she crawled into bed.

Her body still vibrated with need from Max's kiss and his hands as they'd stroked her back and shoulders. His touch had been electric and full of promise. In an odd way, she felt he'd branded her as his. Her fingers slipped between her legs and found her swollen clit. She'd barely touched herself when one of the most intense climaxes she'd ever experienced rocked her. The spasms traveled all the way to her toes. Her back arched, and she cried out in delight.

Audrey wanted more. She wanted Max's hands and mouth on her, wanted his cock buried deep inside. Her fingers worked her clit. It stiffened under her fingers like the miniature penis it was. She imagined Max's mouth on hers again and a string of lush kisses trailing to her breasts. He tongued them and sucked just the way she liked. The way that made her womb contract in delight.

Her other hand found a breast and rolled the hard nipple between thumb and forefinger. She rubbed her clit harder. In her fantasy, Max moved lower on her body and positioned himself between her legs. When he closed his mouth over her sensitive nub, she exploded again, writhing against her hand.

"Holy crap," she moaned. "How am I going to get through two weeks working next to him without dragging him into a broom closet and fucking his brains out?"

"If you're smart, you won't." The wolf sounded smug.

Embarrassment flooded her. She'd forgotten all about her new sidekick who, apparently, missed nothing. *"I guess you were, uh, watching me?"*

A whuffling sound that might've been lupine laughter sounded inside her mind. *"Better than that. When one of us comes, both of us do. Just wait until you're inside me, and we have sex with his wolf. You'll be amazed."*

"Stop it. We probably won't even have sex with him as a human. I'm sure he's not a shifter. Christ! He's the California governor. People have to go through extensive background checks. They'd never have allowed a shifter to run for office. He took his oath six months after the government decreed all of us needed to go to prison."

"I know what I know. You'll trust me more as time goes by."

Audrey's eyes felt heavy. She closed them, and an image of Max danced in the darkness. She started to lecture herself on how it would be really stupid to get involved with him but gave it up for a lost cause. She could have the strongest intentions in the world, but once he trained his incredible blue gaze on her, she wouldn't have the strength to resist.

She considered just taking personal time off to cover her last two weeks. She had more than enough hours accrued to cover it. *If I did that, I could leave tomorrow night.* She mapped out the possibility but ran into a major stumbling block.

I couldn't do that to Max. He needs me. At least this way, there'll be time for Human Resources to find a temp I can train.

Max sat in the shielded upstairs study with Johannes picking over the remains of dinner. Johannes had been busy at the vid feed, so Max worked through e-mails and documents on his wrist computer while he ate.

"It's nearly time," he said, glancing at an antique grandfather clock. "What are you up to over there?"

Johannes looked up. The skin around his eyes looked haggard, probably from worry. "Take a few deep breaths, friend."

Max straightened from where he'd been slumped in his chair. "What?"

"I hacked into Audrey's personal vid feed, the one from her apartment." Johannes's intense gaze didn't waver.

Max launched himself from his chair and flew across the room. He grabbed Johannes's arm and peered at the wall screen. "Tell me."

"The last couple of nights, she's been digging up intel on the shifter underground."

"Not possible. You must be mistaken."

"Max." Johannes pried his hand off his arm. "It's all right there. Look." He clicked a few keys, and the display flared to life.

"Shit." A dull, lead weight settled in Max's chest as he studied the screen. She'd had to confine herself to non-sensitive links, but she'd done a fair job sleuthing, nonetheless.

"You know what this probably means." Johannes's voice was harsh, fury just beneath the surface.

Max nodded. "The timing is too close to be a coincidence. She's probably not the one trying to kill me, but it's likely she's linked to them. Shit. Shit. Shit." He sank into a nearby chair and pounded its arm with a closed fist. "Goddammit." He nursed his reddened fist.

"There's got to be some other explanation," his wolf piped up.

"Like what?"

"Something. If she were our enemy, I'd have sensed it." He paused. *"It's breaking the rules, but I could talk with her wolf."*

"No." Johannes jumped into the conversation. He'd apparently figured out Max and his wolf were talking and focused his magic to listen in. *"We're not compounding one wrong thing with a second."*

Privately, Max thought it was a good idea. The world had turned upside down since shifters developed the rules they lived by. Audrey's animal could yield some important clues. He filed the notion for action later when Johannes wasn't close enough to listen in.

"Enough of this." Max waved a hand at the wall screen. "Do what you need to, so we can funnel into the meeting. It starts in three minutes."

～

IT WAS CLOSING on eleven when the get-together ended, and Johannes sent the vid feed into sleep mode. He leaned back in his chair and rubbed his eyes with his fingers.

"I suppose it's a relief we know who's after me," Max muttered. "What O'Hare said about me being a traitor finally makes sense. It's also why the assailants knew about me."

Johannes grunted and sat upright. "Yes and no. I'm really pissed it's our own people. And to find out there are seven loosely-affiliated splinter groups scattered around the globe makes it even worse."

"Why? You mentioned that as a possibility earlier, so it can't have come as a total shock."

Johannes shrugged. "Yeah, I may have mentioned it, but I hoped it wasn't true. Plus, I had no idea there'd be so many of them. Damn it." His mouth curled into a disgusted moue. "The fucking, meddling U.S. government did more harm than they ever imagined with their ill-conceived edict—especially when every other industrialized nation jumped on the bandwagon and copied it." His eyes glittered dangerously. "This whole fiasco has turned us against ourselves. You do realize we'll have to kill our own to burrow our way out."

"Maybe not." Max steepled his fingers and rested his chin on them. A headache throbbed dully behind one eye; he ignored it. "How about if you and I have a, um, discussion with their leadership now that we know who they are."

An incredulous look spread over Johannes's face. "Are you mad? They want to kill you, and you're just going to sashay into their midst, big as you please."

Max shrugged. "Maybe I'm too tired to be rational, but I've always believed in meeting things head on. We could bring half a dozen of us or a dozen. That should make them think twice about shooting me pointblank." He pushed heavily to his feet. "I'm going to bed. I have a mother of a headache."

Max stopped when he got to the door and turned. "I understand why they'd be suspicious—of everything. For Christ's sake, they went into hiding and then watched as things went from bad to worse. They have to blame someone."

"It shouldn't be us." Johannes spat the words out. "We're trying to help, for God's sake."

"Yes, but they don't know that. They've been out of the communication loop since they went dark. You should turn in. It's late."

"I want to do more sleuthing. There should be electronic

footprints if Audrey is linked to the shifter groups we found out about tonight."

Max smiled sadly. "Thanks. Best of luck."

Johannes nodded curtly. "Never fear. I'll let you know what I find. Keep in mind, though, if I don't find anything it could just mean she covered her tracks well."

Max didn't answer. The thought of Audrey being involved in a plot against him made his soul ache. He walked down the hall to his suite of rooms and went through his nightly ritual on autopilot. Feeling like warmed over cat piss, he crawled into bed and used the voice control module to kill the lights.

"Well?" his wolf asked.

"Well, what?"

"Do you want me to find her wolf?"

Max engaged in a momentary struggle with his conscience. At the time shifters had drawn up a covenant to live by back in the Middle Ages, the rule against animals communicating directly with one another made good sense. The bond animals were hard enough to control. The fear had been that they'd band together, take over the partnership, and do something ill-advised that might target shifters for death. Their animal halves ran on instinct, not intellect. With their immense physical prowess, they tended to kill first if they felt threatened, and ask questions later, not unlike vigilante groups. The shifter bond was actually an unbeatable combination— so long as the human had the upper hand.

Max squeezed his eyes shut. Audrey's lovely face floated in the darkness. He tried to harden his heart but only ended up feeling sick at the possibility of her betrayal.

"Yes," he hissed. *"Go for it. Be discreet, goddammit. I don't want to have to justify this decision to Johannes."*

～

WHEN DAWN LIGHTENED THE ROOM, Max chucked the covers aside.

He'd hardly slept but hadn't felt like getting up to chip away at the mountain of work waiting for him, either. There'd been no word from his wolf. The animals had an in-between place where they roamed when they weren't paired with a human or were simply taking a short vacation from the partnership to commune with their own kind. He'd always suspected the animals relished the moments they had to themselves.

Max dragged his wrist computer off the bedside table and clicked a few keys. No word from Johannes, but that might mean a lot of things. One of Johannes's favorite sayings was: bad news is best delivered in person.

No time like the present to find out.

Max got out of bed and padded into the bathroom. The hot water jets had a salutary effect. It didn't take him long to shower, dry off, and dress for the day. He headed toward the kitchen and the smells of coffee and breakfast, which meant Johannes was awake.

Max burst into the kitchen. He couldn't get the words out, so he just looked at Johannes, his face mute with misery.

"I didn't find a thing."

The tiny animal with sharp claws that had taken up residence in Max's guts relaxed its hold a tiny bit. "I know you were thorough."

"Very."

"Where do we go from here?"

"Your plate's on the table." Johannes took a long swallow of coffee. "We either set up a meeting with the leaders of the splinter groups—" he hesitated and snagged Max's gaze with his own "—or we start killing them. In terms of Audrey—"

"Killing our own is a violation of the covenant." Max interrupted because he didn't want to talk about Audrey. He slid into his customary seat.

"They broke it first." Johannes carried his own food to the table and sat.

Max shoveled food into his mouth. Johannes was an excellent cook, but the ham and eggs tasted like paste. He wasn't hungry but ate anyway. Ideas flowed better if his stomach was full. Johannes's logic was incontrovertible, but killing other shifters went against the grain. "We'll think of something," he mumbled around a mouthful of eggs. "Just give me a little time."

"I'd hurry it up." Johannes shot Max a meaningful glance from across the table.

"Yeah. No point in waiting for them to strike again, is there?"

"No. Back to Audrey. If I were you, I'd stay away from her until we know for sure."

"You're not me."

"Be reasonable." Compulsion ran beneath the words.

Max swallowed sudden fury so he wouldn't jump to his feet and drive a fist into Johannes's face. "I know you care about me, but do not ever use your magic to try to control what I do. Not now. Not ever." Max balled his hands into tight fists. "I'm conflicted enough about her as it is."

"I'm sorry. Point taken about my magic. Truth will rise to the surface. It always does, just like day-old news. Finish your food, and we'll go to work."

AUDREY HURRIED TO HER DESK, almost too keyed up to think. Her wolf had told her Max's wolf paid them a visit during the night, but she was less than forthcoming when Audrey asked what he wanted. No matter what her wolf said, she still didn't believe Max could possibly be a shifter. Audrey nodded to herself.

The wolf nailed it when she said it would take time for us to trust each other.

Maybe that was just a cock-and-bull story the wolf made up to try to push her into Max's arms. The more Audrey thought about it, the more sense it made, especially since the wolf hadn't been able to come up with a reason for the alleged visit. She snickered.

Alleged. I'm starting to think like a lawyer. I really do need to get out of this place.

She'd been up early and gone by the credit machine and then the pawn shop. A thick wad of black market cash was stuffed inside her bra. It seemed the safest place until she could take it home and put it with her other cash in a carved oak box with a hollow bottom. Still, it made her nervous. She glanced at the half mirror mounted on the wall beside her desk and checked for telltale bulges.

Nope. I'm fine.

Audrey settled at her desk and began sorting the incoming mail, messages, and documents for Max. It was just past seven. He generally showed up between seven and nine, depending on what he had scheduled for the day. Fingers working automatically, she brought up his schedule on her wrist computer. No early meetings today, which should mean he'd be in any time. Her heart beat faster at the prospect of seeing him again.

At eight on the dot, he came through the elevator doors, nodded to her, and walked past her desk. He looked so fatigued, her heart ached for him. What the hell had happened last night? Dark circles etched beneath his eyes, and his jaw was set in grim lines.

"Max? Are you all right?"

"Just send me what I need to do through the vid feed." He disappeared through the stairwell door, heading for his office one floor up.

Tears pricked beneath her lids. Had last night been a dream? What about lunch yesterday when he'd leaned so close his heady scent enveloped her? Or dinner two nights before? She swallowed hard.

"Go after him."

"Leave me alone. I'd like to exit this job with my dignity intact. It's obvious he—"

"For the love of Fenrir, god of wolves, go after him. Don't give me a raft of excuses."

A tear rolled down one cheek. She brushed it away. The foyer was mercifully empty, but that could change in a matter of seconds. She gazed at her hands, poised over her keyboard.

What should she do? Her finely honed resolve to keep her relationship with Max professional went to hell last night when she let him kiss her.

I had the strength to walk away from him last night.

But that's not what I want.

It may not matter what I want if he's changed his mind, a different inner voice sniped.

Her wrist computer vibrated, followed by Max's voice on its intercom function. "Audrey, where's today's work?"

"Sorry, sir. Coming right up." She made certain to keep her face out of the camera's range so he wouldn't see she was crying.

Too bad I can't gather up a stack of papers and walk them in to him.

"Get up, and go to his office." The wolf sounded exasperated—and furious.

Because it jived with what she wanted to do—and she wasn't getting anything done anyway—Audrey stood. She'd always believed it was best to address things directly and get them over with. This wasn't any different. She could ask if she'd been mistaken about his intentions. If he said yes, she'd nurse her wounds and find a way to live with the disappointment.

Somehow.

Shoulders square, head high, she mounted the stairs that led to his office. Johannes hadn't been with him today. Or maybe he was and had simply taken the elevator to the top floor, skipping hers. A ray of hope forced its way into her heart. Max could have done the same thing. He'd chosen a route to his office that led past her desk. Surely it meant something. Her heart beat against her chest wall so hard, she could barely breathe. She crossed the carpeted hall on shaky legs, wishing she hadn't worn high heels, and knocked softly on his closed door.

It flew open, and she stood face to face with Johannes. So he was still shadowing Max. "What do you want?" he barked, sounding menacing.

"Oh, let her in," Max said. "While you're at it, how about if you leave for a few minutes."

Audrey shifted from foot to foot. This wasn't going anything like she'd planned, but then she hadn't counted on Johannes and his protective streak. He'd told her he'd die for Max, or something very similar. Apparently, he took his bodyguard responsibilities seriously. Gazing at the fire in his green eyes cowed her, but she was damned if she'd let him know that.

Johannes turned so he could see both her and Max. "I don't think that's a very good idea, sir."

"Well, I do. Out." Max rose to his feet. "You can stand right outside if it makes you feel better."

"With the door open."

"No, with it closed." Max sank back into his chair, intense blue gaze fixed right on her. He looked wary, as if he didn't trust her.

After a lengthy pause, the door finally clicked shut with Johannes on its other side.

Audrey inhaled raggedly. Words tumbled out almost of their own accord. "Sorry to intrude, and just tell me to go back downstairs if I'm out of line, but I had to see you."

She blew out a breath, sucked in another, and hurried on before her courage failed. "Was last night just a sham? Did you change your mind?" She held herself like a tightly wound spring and waited for his answer.

Max closed his hands around the edge of his desk; his knuckles whitened. "Why have you been researching the shifter underground?"

She clanked her teeth together so hard they ached. Her first thought was to deny it, but lying didn't sit well. "How would you know about that? It wasn't on work time."

"It doesn't matter how I know. Just answer the question, Miss Westen."

"I can't."

"Are you more comfortable talking this way?"

Her eyes widened. Blood roared in her ears.

"I know you can hear me," Max went on. *"Don't bother to deny it."*

Joy, brighter than any sun, jolted her. If he could speak into her mind, he had to be a shifter. She knew they could communicate telepathically because of her father. Tears streamed down her face. *"I don't want to deny it. This means my wolf was right."*

"What was she right about? Tell me why you can shift. You shouldn't be able to." Max got to his feet.

"I got the drug, the serum, from the black market. I wanted to be one of you, so I could help us. It's why I resigned. The underground needs help. I figured that out from all those documents we went over. And I first shifted right after that, so..."

"Whoa, whoa." Hope blazed from his eyes.

"Sorry, I know I was babbling, but it's just such a relief to tell someone who might help me figure out how things work. And it means I don't have to hide who I am from you, which means—"

"Yes, darling. It means all those things."

She didn't understand quite how Max covered the distance between them so quickly. He folded his arms around her shaking body. He stroked her hair and her back and murmured nonsensical words into her ear until she relaxed against him.

"It's the shifter groups in hiding that are trying to kill me," he explained, talking softly into her ear. "We finally figured at least that much out. They blame me and the underground for the escalation in enmity and all the shifter deaths. When Johannes hacked into your vid feed and saw where you'd been, we were afraid you were part of them."

She moved back an inch or two and looked up at him. "I could never do that. I've been in love with you for a long time."

"Good to hear since I'm falling in love with you."

He smiled, and her heart took wing.

"But it's far more than that, Audrey darling." He bent close and whispered, "If our wolves are right, you're my mated one." He kissed her forehead tenderly. "All I know is I've never felt such an intense attraction for anyone."

"Me, either." She nestled against his body.

Warmth, relief she'd trusted her instincts, and a liquid heat between her thighs vied for ascendency. She wanted to stay in his arms forever. It was the rightest place she'd ever known. She turned her face up, and Max kissed her, gently at first but with increasing urgency as his hands trailed down her back and snugged her against his body. His cock jutted into the junction between her thigh and stomach. She pressed against him, breath coming fast, tightened her arms, and opened her mouth to his kiss.

A soft tap sounded on the door. Max pulled away. "It's Johannes. I'd know his knock anywhere. We'll have all the time in the world to savor each other." He kissed the tip of her nose and called, "Come in."

Johannes came through the door, closing it behind him. Max quirked a brow. Johannes nodded, relief obvious on his face and in the relaxed set of his shoulders. "She told the truth."

Audrey turned her head to look at Johannes. "Of course I did. I always do. You can tell things like that?"

He nodded. *"I'm a cat shifter. We have different gifts than you do. One is sensitivity to falsehoods."* He grinned. It transformed his face. "I suppose the two of you will want to retire to our house for the rest of the day."

Max grinned back. "Maybe the rest of our lives."

"But we can't just leave," she protested. "The office is open. One of us needs to be here. There're probably people piling up downstairs."

"Ah, the voice of reason." Max tightened his arms around her. "How about a compromise? We'll work until noon, leave for lunch, and just not come back."

"Good plan," Johannes said.

Both the men looked at her, waiting for her assent. Heat crept from her chest to her face. "Guess since it was my idea to keep the office manned, I'll have to agree. First thing I'm going to do is call Personnel and see if they can send a temp in at noon." She peeked at her wrist computer and felt her blush deepen. "It's going to be the longest three and a half hours of my life."

Johannes laughed. "Speak for yourself. I'll be the one babysitting your prospective mate, *er*, lover."

"Babysitting?" Max let go of Audrey, socked Johannes in the arm, and laughed right along with him.

"Before I go downstairs." Audrey looked at Max, her mind racing. "A little while ago you said something about the shifters blaming you and the underground for how bad things are." Concerned they might be overheard, she switched to telepathic speech. *"Are you connected to the shifter underground?"*

"Perceptive of you, Miss Westen. I'm the head of it."

Max danced a small jig around his office. He couldn't remember the last time he'd been truly happy. Maybe he'd never been happy like this, where joy spilled from every pore and made the air in the room glow.

"*Why didn't you tell me?*" he asked his wolf.

"*Audrey's wolf and I discussed it. In the end, we decided it would be best to stay out of things unless we absolutely had to intervene. We couldn't imagine a mated pair walking away from one another.*"

"*You could've said something.*"

"Your electronic in-basket is filling up, judging from all those dings," Johannes noted, mercifully not mentioning that Max and his wolf had broken the shifter covenant. Of course, it was possible the wolf had shielded his words.

"Oh, who gives a fuck?" Max loped over to where Johannes stood next to a window and grabbed his arms. He lowered his voice to a whisper. "Once I'm positive we're mates—and I'll know when we shift spontaneously once we start to make love—you'll perform the ritual mating ceremony. Maybe even later tonight."

"It would be my pleasure." A soft smile illuminated Johannes's face as he whispered back. "More than a pleasure, an honor. It's been over a hundred years since I've joined a mated shifter pair."

Max nodded, gave Johannes a quick hug, and stepped back, but not so far he couldn't keep his voice soft. "I know. I felt the same way when I joined Kate and Devon. It gave me hope our kind wouldn't die out."

Johannes's smile disappeared. "We won't. I don't care if we have to kill every last one of those bastards who hung us out to dry when they penned that edict. Plus the shifters who've turned into Benedict Arnolds."

"We can't kill all of them. It's not practical. We need to make them see reason, repeal the damned thing, and talk sense into our own kind. Not just here but around the world."

Johannes rolled his eyes. "You've turned into quite the politician. Maybe you've overstayed your welcome here."

"I don't know about that. Feels like I'm just hitting my stride."

"Spoken like a man with a perpetual hard-on."

Max patted the front of his trousers and rearranged himself. "Okay. Fine. I'm going to try to make a dent in whatever Audrey sent up here. I can't wait until it's time to leave. Once we get home—"

"You don't have to tell me. I'll ward everything and try not to jack off too many times while the smell of your heat permeates the whole house."

"Maybe you could wash your hands in between times and make us a special dinner."

Johannes laughed. "That could probably be arranged."

The rest of the morning actually went far quicker than Max imagined it would. A group of teachers, concerned over escalating violence on campus, took up over an hour. Johannes ushered them out and said, "It's time."

Max shrugged into his jacket, stuffed a few things into his briefcase, and powered down the vid feed. "When I took this job, I told myself I was doing it to," he lowered his voice, "help us. Maybe it's an illusion, but I think I'm improving the quality of life for everyone in the state, at least in some small ways."

"You've always been a man of integrity. How could you bring less than your best to anything? Come on, let's go get your mate."

Max floated down the stairs and pushed through the door into the reception area. Audrey smiled shyly. A spot of color bloomed on each cheek. "Just let me close things down here. Human Resources is sending a gal to hold down the fort. She'll be here after lunch."

"Anything I can help with?" Max asked. Heart hammering against his ribs, he felt like a nervous adolescent about to embark on his first date.

Audrey shook her head and rose from her seat. She was lovely. Today she wore a dark green wool suit and a black blouse that looked like silk. Her long, shapely legs were encased in nylon stockings; shiny, black high-heeled pumps made her calves look divine. She cocked her head to one side. "Should I follow you with my car?"

"I'll drive with you," Max said.

Her smile broadened. "I was hoping you'd say that. I've been more than a little distracted." She laughed. "Not that having you inches from me is going to help."

Johannes called the elevator. The door opened, and Max gestured all of them through.

She thinks she's been distracted. It will be a blooming miracle if we make it home in one piece.

They did the same thing they'd done the previous night and drove to her car a couple of levels deeper in the garage. She tossed her things into the trunk, and he helped her in, hands lingering on her arm and shoulder before he moved around to his side of the car.

"I was thinking about how we could use this time," she said once they were underway.

"I love your efficiency, but I'm not sure we need it right now."

"Of course we do. You can tell me some basic things I need to know about being a shifter."

"Sure." Max loosened his tie and laid a proprietary hand on her leg. "You feel so good. I can't wait to get you out of those clothes."

She slapped his hand playfully away. "See. This is why I thought we needed something to focus on. I won't be much of a driver if all I'm thinking about is dragging you onto a bed and fucking your brains out."

"You don't need to be much of a driver," he pointed out, placing his hand higher. "The car does most of the thinking for you."

"Yes, but it can't avoid accidents. The newer ones have sensors, but this one doesn't." She wriggled beneath his touch. "I need a basic primer on shifters. Consider it something like *Shifter 101.*"

"Anything in particular?"

She tossed her hands in the air, palms up. "I don't know squat. You could begin anywhere."

Max thought about it. "Let's talk about mating and what it means if you're my mated one and I'm yours."

"My wolf thinks we are. How will we know?" Her brows drew together, giving her a studious look.

Max loved looking at her. He drank in every aspect of her face, from hair to chin line and then moved his gaze downward. Full breasts pushed against the filmy fabric of her top. Her nipples were clearly visible. His cock reacted violently, pressing against the front of his trousers with a vengeance.

She moved his hand off her thigh and giggled. "You're not answering me, and you're practically panting over there."

"Observant, Miss Westen. It's one of the many things I appreciate about you. I'm having a hard time thinking." He flicked at the bulge of his erection. "Men are like that. If one head's working, the other one isn't." He sucked in a steadying breath. "We will know because once we begin to make love, we'll shift spontaneously."

Her eyes widened. "Really? What happens to our lovemaking then?"

Heat roared through him. It took all his willpower not to tell the nav system to pull over to the curb. "We make love as wolves. Then we shift back and make love as humans. Coupling in both our forms cements our bond."

"Tell me more about what it means to be mated. Is it like being married?"

"Yes, but ever so much more. Our kind mates for life—and we live for a very long time. It's a binding of souls that lasts through this life and all lives to come."

Her eyes filled with tears. "I love how that sounds. How much farther to your house?"

Max glanced out the windshield. He hadn't been paying attention to anything but Audrey. "Not far. Another half mile or so."

"Is there a ceremony?"

"Yes. Johannes will perform it once we're certain." Max started to tell her the ritual involved Johannes standing by while they coupled as wolves but decided to wait on that detail. He didn't want to scare her off. Once they'd had sex, they'd both be so entranced with one another, caught up in the mate bond, she wouldn't care if the entire state of California stood by and watched while they fucked.

"You know." She blushed deeply, rose shading to crimson. "I've been half in love with you since the first time I saw you on the vid feed before you took office. I voted for you because I wanted you close to me."

A warm glow began in his belly and radiated outward. Max wanted her to love him as much as he'd ever wanted anything. "Now you tell me. Why'd you wait so long? What's it been? Eighteen months?"

She shrugged, looking sheepish. "I was still married. I needed to get out of that entanglement. Beyond my initial infatuation, though, I respect the work you've done. Maybe more than almost anyone else, I know what a hard worker you are and how seriously you take your oath of office. You needed my help. I guess I thought I'd wait until your term was up—or something."

"Turn in here." Max pointed and worked his wrist computer to open the gates. She ferried her car through. "What if I'd been reelected?"

"I don't know if I could've waited another four years. Where do you want me to park?"

"In front of the house is fine. Johannes will take care of putting your car away."

"Should I leave my wrist computer?"

"He's a wizard. He'll figure things out. Don't worry about your bag or briefcase, either." Max got out of the car and went around to open her door. "Come here." He held out his hands. "We've waited long enough."

She took his hands and let him tug her gently from the car. He closed his arms around her and bent his head. "Darling," he murmured, just before he kissed her.

Max reveled in the feel of her mouth beneath his. Her lips were full and firm, and she opened her mouth under his almost instantly. When he sank his tongue into her mouth, she sucked hungrily on it. He felt her nipples, hard where they pressed against his chest. And something else too.

He broke away from the kiss and patted the front of her blouse. "What's this?"

She grinned rakishly. "A wad of black market cash. I was planning a getaway, remember?"

"Good, you know how to finesse these things. We use the black market for a lot of our operations."

Johannes pulled up behind Audrey's car. He flashed Max a thumbs up sign.

"Ready to go inside?" Max asked.

"If I were any readier, I'd bend over one of those planters."

"Nice visual. I'll bet you have a great ass. In fact I know you do. I've felt it." He tucked her hand under his elbow and led her up the stairs. The door clicked open. Max assumed Johannes had taken care of it from his vantage point in the driveway. "After you, my dear."

Audrey walked into the house. "Oh my God," she breathed. "I had no idea you lived in a museum."

~

THE POLISHED MAHOGANY floor of the foyer opened into a great room decorated with plush hand-woven carpets, Louis the Fourteenth furniture, and overstuffed leather easy chairs. An ornate marble fireplace took up one end of the huge room. Audrey shook her head. "I can look at all this later. The only thing I really want to look at now is you."

"That's the nicest thing anyone's ever said to me. Come on upstairs. Unless you'd like to bring some food or refreshments up with us."

She shook her head. "No. I'm feeling nervous as it is. This shifter stuff is still really, really new."

He kissed her and took her hand. "I'll take care of you, Audrey. I'll never let anyone hurt you or anything bad happen to you." Max's voice vibrated with emotion as he led her up a carpeted stairway that hugged a wainscoted wall.

"Don't make promises you can't keep." Her throat was so thick, it was hard to talk. Love coursed through her, so rich with promise it made every other emotion pale by comparison.

"I won't. One more flight. Okay, all the way to the end of the hall." He moved in front of her, opened the door, and scooped her into his arms.

"What? You're carrying me across the threshold? I thought you were supposed to do that at the front door."

"I was afraid once I got my hands on that much of you, we'd never make it all the way up here." He set her back on her feet. His hands shook slightly as he pushed her jacket off her shoulders. He started on the buttons of her blouse.

"Wait. Let me get out of these heels." She toed first one shoe off, then the other. "Better. I'm shaky enough." She held out her arms.

He wrapped her in his and kissed her. Even more than his earlier kisses, this one held heat and need. For the first time, she caught a glimpse of the emotional depth he kept under wraps.

She slid her hands down his back and cupped his high, firm ass, pulling him as close to her as she could. He groaned and deepened their kiss. She felt his erection sandwiched between them. It jerked against her body. Her breasts ached. Her thighs were awash in fluid. She told herself to slow down, that they had all the time they'd ever need, but her body didn't see it that way.

She broke away from their kiss, breathless. "We can get fancy with this later. Right now, there are way too many clothes in the way." She reached for the buttons on his shirt, barely able to make her fingers obey because they shook so badly. He shrugged out of his suit coat and then the shirt she'd managed to unbutton. Audrey sucked in a breath. She ran fingertips down his bronze skin. He had perfectly muscled arms and shoulders and a hard, flat stomach with planes of muscle disappearing into the waistband of his trousers. Fine blond hairs sprinkled around his nipples. She moved in and licked one, gratified by his sudden intake of breath.

"Fair's fair." He found the buttons of her blouse again and pushed it off her shoulders. It slithered to the floor. He plucked the black market cash from between her breasts. "Hey, a tip!" He tossed the money on a table.

She laughed. "Hold up there, sweetie. You need to earn it first."

He unhooked her bra and tugged it off her shoulders. It fell to the floor atop her blouse. A look of wonder washed over his face, and he filled his hands with her breasts, growling low in the back of his throat. "Beautiful. You're exquisite." He bent his head and traded his hands for his mouth, kissing and suckling her just like in her fantasy. Streams of sensation made her legs weak.

Audrey wriggled and pressed her thighs together. They were slick with her arousal. "I'm not sure how much longer I'll be able to stand up." She undid his belt and started on the fastenings of his pants. "I hope you have condoms," she blurted, "because I don't."

He let go of the nipple he'd been tonguing. "We don't need them."

"Huh?" She ran her hands up his torso. His skin was amazing. Silky and electric, it sent bolts of desire from her fingertips to her pussy.

"Shifters don't get human diseases, and I control when my seed impregnates. Enough discussion. I need to get my shoes off," he said thickly, his voice harsh with craving her.

She glanced down. Wingtips. "Here, let me." She knelt before him and untied both shoes. He balanced with a hand on her shoulder while she worked them off one at a time. When she raised her head, she closed her mouth over the bulge in his pants, breathing heat and desire through the fabric.

A feral sound escaped him. Max plunged his hands into her hair, scattering pins and clips. She finished undoing his trousers, gave a tug, and they pooled on the floor. The outline of his cock through cream-colored silk shorts made her heart beat so fast, she was afraid she might pass out. He let go of her hair long enough to push his underwear out of the way.

His cock was huge and amazing. Wonderfully shaped, it curved toward her invitingly. A single drop of fluid glistened on the glans. She rubbed it around the sensitive head with a fingertip and then took him into her mouth, nibbling and sucking. Her own climax was so close, she thought she might come just from sucking on him.

"Audrey, sweetheart." He pulled her upright. "I'll come if you keep doing that, and I want to come inside your pussy—at least this first time." His eyes gleamed with hunger. His breath came fast. He fumbled with her skirt. It slid down her hips. "Help me with your stockings."

She pushed ineffectually at them and then walked to the bed. Perched on the edge, she shinnied out of her nylons. The only thing left was a lacy, pink thong.

With a roar, Max dove across the room, landing practically on top of her. He covered her body with his and kissed her with a vengeance. The feel of his skin against hers was incredible and thrilling. Wherever he touched her came alive with desperate, aching need. She ground her body against him. Release was close, so close.

He reached between them and ripped the thong out of the way. "Sorry, sorry," he murmured. "I can't wait any longer. I have to be inside you."

Audrey wrapped her legs around his waist and her arms around his shoulders and hung on. His cock slid into her in a long, delicious heave. That was all it took. As he hit bottom, she convulsed around him. To keep from screaming, she bit his shoulder and then kissed him.

He moved his mouth away from hers and looked down from where he balanced on his arms. "Yes, sweet girl, come for me. I wish you could see yourself. You're glowing."

Her orgasm barely took a bite out of her need. She moved her hips lazily. "More." His face was so beautiful, she couldn't tear her eyes away.

"I'll give you all the more you want." He withdrew. His cock glistened with her fluids. "Turn over, darling, on your hands and knees."

Audrey flipped over and felt him sink inside her again. He closed a hand over her swollen nub and rubbed as he drove his cock into her. Another climax rose to the surface, rolling in on the waves of the last one. She was close, almost there, when he crowed. "Open your eyes, we're shifting. We'll finish making love as wolves."

$\mathcal{M}$ ax's claws dug into the soft fabric of the bedclothes. He was probably ripping the shit out of them, but he didn't care. From his vantage point behind her, he watched Audrey transform into a stunning black and gray timber wolf with a lush pelt. He felt his own transformation. Felt his penis develop a bulb at the base that swelled inside her vulva, binding them together.

He forced himself to wait until the transformation was complete. This coupling would count as the one in animal form, but not if it happened before they were fully wolves. His cock was so hard, it ached. He'd been on the edge of coming for a long time, but he'd wanted to bring her to a second climax. The transformation only took moments, but they lasted an eternity. Finally, he let himself go. His climax rocked him to the pads of his feet. He tossed back his head and howled and then buried his teeth in the junction between her neck and shoulder.

Audrey howled right along with him. Her vulva quivered. He rocked his cock deeper inside her. Her muscles clenched around him and clenched again. He kept on moving to extend her orgasm. He wanted her to come a thousand times. His mate. His woman. She would never want for anything. Ever. He would see to it.

Ecstasy didn't come close to describing his delight. Earlier, part of him had been lost in the wonder of her body, but another part was waiting for them to shift. It was only when he stopped worrying about it—and trying to control things—that nature had taken over.

Long minutes passed before her body stopped quivering. She wriggled her butt against him.

"We're stuck like this for a while," he told her.

"I thought it might be something like that," she murmured. *"Oh, Max. I don't care if we're stuck like this forever. Maybe I do. I love you so much. I want to be able to turn around and hold you and kiss you."*

"Soon, darling. My love. My mate." He growled, surprised by the possessive note.

"At first I kept waiting for us to shift, then I got so caught up in wanting you, I guess I sort of forgot all about it."

"Which is why it finally happened." He moved inside her, testing things. It seemed he was a little smaller. Maybe he'd be able to slip out. It would be nice to get their paws on the floor. The bed was far too soft.

"Oh my God, you're white." She craned her neck around to look at him. *"I saw a white paw, but all of you is white. And your pelt is gorgeous."*

"I'm a Russian wolf. All of us are white. Helps us hunt in winter—which lasts damn near all year."

"If we have children—"

"Not if, when." He heaved backward and tugged himself out of her body. *"Come on down to the floor. You can look at me all you like."*

She took him at his word, padding around him and licking and sniffing. *"You're even more handsome as a wolf than you are as a human, and that's saying something."* She licked his snout.

Max didn't know how to respond. Emotion thrummed through him. He shifted and said, *"Now you. I want to hold you against my human body."*

The air around her shimmered as she shifted.

"I wasn't done," his wolf protested.

"You'll get another opportunity soon enough at the mating ceremony."

"I was right," his wolf boasted, sounding insufferably smug.

"I should listen to you more often," Max told him. He grinned and drew Audrey's naked body into his arms.

"Truer words were never spoken," the wolf gloated.

"Yours talks to you too?" Audrey looked up at him, her hazel eyes aglow with joy.

Max laughed. "You betcha." He ran his hands down the silk of her skin. "Ready for one more round, or would you like a break? Something to eat or drink or a bath?"

"Maybe a drink of water. I started to ask you this before. If we have children, what will they look like?"

"Probably timber wolves like you. The white color and long coat should be recessive, but I'm not certain about that. We'll just have to produce a few and find out." He grinned. "Are you sure you don't want juice or wine or beer or liquor? I've got some stellar Irish whiskey from the eighteen hundreds."

"Later. Didn't you say we needed to make love both ways before we were, uh, mated?"

"You came in both forms. So the bond's complete on your side."

Her eyes danced with mischief. "Looks like you owe me an orgasm." She closed her hands over his stiffening cock. "How do you want me, and how can we keep from shifting?"

"Frontal sex works pretty well. Or you could finish what you started with your mouth." He kissed her forehead and her eyelids. "Depends if you want to come again. Of course, we could do simultaneous oral."

"I feel like a kid in a candy store. I want it all. I want you in my mouth and in my pussy and in my hands. I don't think I'll ever get tired of looking at you or feeling you against me."

"I love you, Audrey." He covered her mouth with his.

She returned his kiss with a joy that filled his soul. Finally, after all this time, he was complete. An empty place inside him would never be empty again. She hadn't been a shifter long enough to fully appreciate what that meant. He maneuvered them back toward the bed, never breaking their kiss. Her tongue sparred with his. His cock throbbed between them, anxious to bury itself inside her again.

Audrey must have felt it because she trailed kisses down his body, leaving a track of liquid fire. Before she could kneel in front of him, he lifted her onto the bed and lay next to her. She tongued a trail down his chest and stomach. When her mouth closed over his cock, it felt exquisite. Bolts of pure lust radiated from his dick to his fingers and toes, his body a lightning rod for pleasure. She nibbled with her teeth and pumped his shaft with a hand. Her other hand moved between his legs and pressed right behind his balls.

They snugged against his body. The only thing in the world was Audrey and her knowing mouth and fingers. His cock exploded, alight with burning jets as they raced outward. He came forever, higher than he'd ever been.

She licked and swallowed, finally lifting her mouth from him. "Sweet," she murmured. "I love doing that. I could get hooked on the way you taste and feel in my mouth. Did you know you swell even more right before you come? I didn't think you could get any bigger, but—"

He pulled her up the length of his body and sank his tongue inside her mouth. She tasted of him, and it drove him mad. He felt himself harden again. Her hips pressed rhythmically against him. Erect nipples jabbed into his chest. He put a hand on either side of her face and drew away from their kiss. "Do you want me inside you or my mouth on you?"

"It's a hard choice." A broad grin split her face. "How about mouth—this time."

Max flipped her onto her back and positioned himself so his head was between her legs. He licked her nub experimentally. She buried her hands in his hair and drove her pussy against his face. "Move, goddammit," she growled.

He took her clit into his mouth and sucked while plunging

fingers inside her pussy. He paid special attention to her G-spot. Audrey moaned and writhed under his touch. When he glanced up, she'd moved her hands to her breasts and was twirling the nipples. Her clit swelled. She had to be close. He sucked harder and worked her pussy with his fingers. Her muscles grabbed his fingers and grabbed again. She was coming. He sucked and licked until her arched back fell onto the mattress.

"Oh my God. That was amazing," she said, panting. "You can do it again whenever you want."

He pulled his fingers out of her and sucked them clean. What a sweet pussy she had. Tight and hot and fragrant. His wolf was damn near incontrollable. He wanted out for another round.

Audrey laughed and held out her arms. He crawled up her body and settled into them. "My wolf wants more. She wants to know when the mating ritual will be."

"After we take a break and eat something."

"Maybe I could rinse off."

"Good idea. I'm right behind you."

AUDREY LEANED against Max as he soaped her with a loofah. "Where do you get all this stuff?" She gestured to the soap, shampoo, and bathing sponges. "I've seen some at the black market, but they're wicked expensive."

"Johannes gets them from a number of black markets. Not all of them are located in the U.S." He sluiced water down her body. "Ready to get out?"

"Not really. I feel like I woke up in a fairy tale. I never want it to end."

"It never will." He turned off the water and drew her close. "You'll never have to worry about anything ever again. I'll take care of you." He grabbed a thick towel and wrapped her in it.

"Do I get to take care of you too?" Audrey was so moved, it was hard to find words.

"Of course, darling. We'll take care of each other." He tossed her a robe. "Let's go downstairs. Johannes should have supper made for us."

"Is it dinnertime already?" She slid into the soft terrycloth and belted it around herself.

"Are you hungry?"

She nodded.

"Then it's dinnertime."

Audrey followed him back to the mansion's first level. The smells from dinner made her mouth water. Feeling like a spectator on a tour, she craned her neck first one way, then the other. The house was so large, it would take weeks to get familiar with the place. She gazed at an array of artwork and sculpture that must've cost a fortune.

"Not that it matters, but you must have a lot of money. California pays you pretty well but not nearly well enough to afford all this." She took his arm once they got to the main floor.

"I've been alive for a long time. And I've done a lot of things."

"You're going to tell me about each of them." Possessiveness burned in every nerve ending. She wanted to know everything about Max.

"Of course I am. Mates have no secrets from each other." He pushed open a swinging door and held it for her.

Johannes leapt to his feet with a warm smile on his face. He strode to her and kissed her forehead. "Welcome to the pack, sister."

"Thank you. Are you really part of a pack with Max? How are shifter packs organized?" Even though she knew it was safe to ask, the questions still felt awkward on her tongue.

"No, I'm a mountain cat. You were right about one thing a few days ago, though. Max and I have known each other for hundreds of years."

"Watch it." Max jabbed Johannes's arm. "She'll start thinking I'm much too old for her."

"How many hundreds?" Audrey was fascinated.

"Never mind," Max murmured. "Dinner smells great. We're ready."

"I'll just bet you are. I could smell the, um, progress of your activities." Johannes leered knowingly. "You're lucky I didn't storm the fortress. I was this close—" he held up his thumb and forefinger "—to joining the fun."

"Really?" Audrey looked from one man to the other. After the intense lovemaking with Max, she couldn't imagine adding anyone to the equation. Not only couldn't she imagine it, she didn't even want to.

"No. I'm joking. We may take some women as a team, but mates are a whole other story. They're definitely a one-on-one proposition." Johannes winked. "Take her into the dining room, Max. I thought we could eat in there tonight, since it's such a special occasion."

Max drew her through a door on the far side of the kitchen. Audrey took a step into the old-fashioned formal dining room and gasped. Tears filled her eyes. A chandelier with too many lighted candles to count illuminated a polished mahogany table set with crystal, china, and silver. A matching sideboard almost groaned under the weight of several dishes.

"This is all for us?" She turned to Max, not trusting herself with more words.

"Yes, love. All for us. It's a rare and wonderful day when one of us finds their mated one. Let me seat you." He pulled out a chair.

She took a closer look at the carved wood and padded seat before she sat. "This looks like an antique."

"Well, it was new when I bought it in the eighteen hundreds. Cost a fortune to ship it over here from Europe. I'm glad you like old things. I've never been able to force myself to get rid of any of the furnishings in this house, even though they're not practical." He took the chair next to hers.

"If I read the regulations right, a lot of these things aren't even legal to own anymore. Like that big bathtub upstairs. They use too much water. Or—" she glanced at the lit fireplace with a log in it crackling merrily "—those. Wood is scarcely available for anything anymore. Burning it is—"

"Spare me, Carrie Nation. I find certain things…comforting. And I have a problem with laws designed to protect me from myself. One of the trees on the estate blew down during a storm last month. The wood isn't any good to anyone, so I'm using it for the occasional fire. It's either that or give it to one of those pulp mills."

Johannes walked into the dining room carrying a bottle of champagne. "What? You haven't served yourselves yet? The food will get cold." He poured the fizzy liquid into cut crystal champagne flutes.

Audrey smiled around a lump in her throat. She still couldn't quite believe her new life. "Here." She got to her feet. "Let me dish up our dinners. I'd feel better if I could be helpful. Truly."

She padded to the sideboard and took silver lids off the serving dishes. "Oh, my." She turned to glance at Johannes over one shoulder. "Come tell me what each of these is."

He set the champagne down and walked to her side. "This one is a lamb casserole with caramelized onions. This is chicken breast in a creamy parmesan sauce. This is orzo with fresh herbs from the garden and a bit of cream. The rest you'd recognize easily."

"Mmph. Looks like I could benefit from some time in the kitchen with you. Never was much of a cook."

"It doesn't matter," Max said. "I'd still love you if you burned water."

"That's only because you'd still have me to cook for you," Johannes teased.

"What do you want?" she asked Max.

"A little of everything."

For a while the only sound was the clink of silver against fine bone china. Audrey didn't realize how hungry she was until she began eating, and then she remembered she hadn't had any lunch and very little for breakfast.

"A toast." Johannes raised a champagne flute. "To a fruitful mating." He cocked his head to one side. "If I'm any judge of things, it's off to a sound start."

She raised her glass and clinked it against the men's. "I'd like to propose a toast as well. To both of you, for being strong and true to our people."

Johannes looked hard at Max. "You got a good one. She's loyal as well as beautiful."

Audrey felt heat rise to her face. "I'm not used to compliments."

"I can tell. Before we have dessert," Johannes asked, "would you like me to formally join you?"

"I thought you'd never ask." Max laid a hand over hers. "Have you had enough to eat for now? The ceremony can take…a while."

She drained her champagne. "Sure. I can eat any time. It's not every day a girl gets married."

Max stood and extended a hand to her. "Come stand by my side in front of the fire."

Johannes followed them and withdrew a smooth, dark stone from his pocket. It was curved and so shiny it reflected light from the fire. "This is a ritual mating stone. As one of twelve elected leaders of the shifter clan, I am authorized to bind mated couples. Hold out your right hands." He made short, deep cuts in the meaty part just beneath the balls of their thumbs and held their hands so the cuts bled into one another.

"Now repeat after me. *Body of my body, blood of my blood, now and forevermore, I shall be yours.*"

"Before you say the words—" Max placed a finger under her chin and tipped it up so her gaze met his "—you need to know this is permanent. It will bind us together throughout eternity in both our forms."

"I understand. You told me something similar earlier." Her heart swelled with emotion. It spilled over in tears. "I love you, Max. I want to be with you through every lifetime I have. Body of my body, blood of my blood, now and forevermore, I shall be yours."

Max repeated the words while looking deep into her eyes. "You're crying." He grazed a knuckle gently over her cheeks.

"It's because I'm happy."

Johannes handed white linen strips to them. "Bind your mating wounds and bury the cloths in a safe place." He elbowed Max. "Ready for the next part?"

Max cleared his throat. "Hopefully. Could you give us a few moments' privacy while I explain what happens next?"

Johannes quirked a brow. "Oho! I'd love to be a fly on that wall, but I shall be a gentleman and retreat to the kitchen where I'll try not to listen. I'm as close as a holler."

CHAPTER 12

"What's all the cloak and dagger stuff?" Audrey wrapped the cloth more firmly around her cut.

Max cringed. Warmth, love, and trust shone from her hazel eyes. He didn't want to do anything to disabuse that trust. He put his arms around her and stroked her hair. "If you were born a shifter you'd know and accept this part. It may sound odd to you since you were raised human."

She pulled back and leveled her no-nonsense gaze at him. "Stop equivocating. Just tell me. It can't be that bad, or there wouldn't be any shifter mated pairs."

He grabbed a breath to buy himself a moment and nodded. "All right. The only thing left to complete the ceremony is we shift and make love as wolves."

Her forehead creased in confusion. "Hey, that doesn't sound so bad. I had a really hot time when we were wolves, and I can tell you my wolf has been chomping at the bit ever since. She's relentless."

"Tell me about it. You should live with mine. On a more serious note, there's one more part. Johannes will be in the room. At a point in the mating, he'll mark our wolves with the ritual mating stone.

It's why one of the elected leaders must be present. We can't mark ourselves."

Her eyes narrowed. "Just in the room, not part of our lovemaking."

Max nodded.

"Whew!" She blew out a breath. "That doesn't sound so bad. With all that buildup, I was afraid I'd have to do something truly perverse."

"Not on my watch, you won't. Now or ever." A savage protectiveness roiled through him. He wanted to crush her against him and never let go.

She clapped her hands together. "Bring it on. I want whatever will make us belong to one another forever."

"I'm really proud of you."

She shot him a grin worthy of the Sirens. "I'm proud of me too, but let's save all this mutual admiration stuff for later. You're looking pretty sexy with your blond hair backlit by the fire. I think I'm ready, plus it will be a relief to let my wolf out to play." Dropping her robe over a chair, she shifted.

"Johannes," Max called.

He strode into the room. "I know. I felt the magic."

Max draped his robe over Audrey's. In moments, he found his wolf form. Audrey nuzzled him and licked his snout. His wolf cock hardened, springing out of its furry sheath. It was a challenge to stand still. He wanted to run and leap and jump and throw back his head and howl at the moon outside the windows.

Audrey put an end to that by sticking her snout between his back legs and licking him shamelessly. Her tongue felt sensual, bringing back memories of her human mouth on his human cock.

The bulb at the base of his cock started to swell. He pulled away from her tongue. *"I can't get too excited or I won't be able to penetrate you."*

"Lots of new rules."

Whuffling with lupine laughter, she turned and planted her butt in front of his snout and then looked at him over her shoulder. In the clearest invitation imaginable, she twisted her tail out of the way, clearing a path.

Max surged forward and grasped her chest between his front paws. His jaws closed around the side of her neck, and he sank his cock inside her vulva. She yipped softly and pushed back against him. The base of his penis expanded, locking them together. Max felt sudden heat lance down his side and understood Johannes had marked him. He'd mark Audrey right below, so the blood could drip and mingle.

Excitement hammered through him. Lupine sex was simple. Enter, swell, come, since wolves lacked hands or mouths for elaborate stroking or foreplay. That she'd spent so much time licking him was unusual, probably reflective of her just learning to shift. And then he stopped thinking. His balls tightened and spewed. Her muscles clamped around him. She whined and then howled her joy as rhythmic contractions cradled him.

Their bodies stilled. Johannes came close. He touched both wounds and made certain some of Audrey's blood entered Max's body. Next he chanted over them in an arcane shifter language. Very few shifters retained knowledge of their ancient tongue. A sense of peace and rightness filled Max. His love for Audrey burned bright in his mind and heart. So this was what the mate bond was like.

Better than my wildest imagination.

When his cock subsided enough to withdraw and Max shifted, Johannes was nowhere in sight.

Good man. Understands it might be awkward until we're dressed.

Audrey watched him shift and then shifted too. He handed her robe to her. He was grinning like an idiot but couldn't stop himself. "The deed is done."

"I feel different, somehow." She gazed into the fire. "It's like there's a slender, glowing thread connecting us. It starts just here—" she pointed at her solar plexus "—and flows across the space between us."

"Yes. I feel it too. Audrey, darling. My love. You've made me the happiest man alive today."

"You couldn't be any happier than me." She melted into his arms.

Sporting a grin as broad as Max's, Johannes came back into the room. "Maybe we could finish dinner. I made chocolate soufflé for dessert. It'll be out of the oven soon. You have to eat it immediately. They don't stay pretty for very long."

They lingered over dessert and port until Audrey started yawning. "You two can stay up, but I'm going to bed. I have no idea what time it is, but I have to be up early."

Max gazed fondly at her. "I'll be upstairs in just a few minutes. I'd like to help Johannes clean things up a bit down here."

"Oh." A hand flew to her mouth. "I should help too. Here." She rose from her chair and began gathering dishes.

"Stop. Brides shouldn't have to do a thing but look fetching on their mating days," Johannes said. "Run along. I promise I won't keep your beloved for too long."

She went to Max's chair, bent her head, and kissed him. "See you soon. I'm so happy. I don't know quite what to do with all the joy. Every time I turn around, I'm crying again."

He rose and put his arms around her. "I love you. Keep the bed warm for me."

"I will. Oh!" She hurried to the carpet in front of the fire and scooped up their white linen bandages from the mating wounds in their thumbs. "What do we need to do with these?"

"I'll take them." Max walked to her. "We'll bury them together in a corner of the yard tomorrow." He gathered dishes as she walked out of the room.

Johannes followed him to the kitchen with another armful. "You don't really have to help, but we could stand a spot of conversation. I got a call from Ryan a little bit ago. After I joined you, but before you shifted back to human."

Something tightened in the pit of Max's stomach. He turned to face Johannes. "Tell me."

"He's worried. He and Devon were working the vid feed. They hacked into some partial feeds. Looks as if there will be another attempt on your life. The splinter shifter groups are pissed because you've eluded them twice now."

"What? Is this sort of a third time's a charm deal?" Max asked. Johannes shrugged. "Never mind. I shouldn't joke. Do you have details?"

"Some. You're scheduled to be at a press conference tomorrow afternoon."

"Yes, it's in the Capitol Rotunda at two."

"You're not going, but don't tell anyone until the last minute. Something you ate at lunch made you sick. You're in the john puking."

Max bit down hard and clenched his jaw. "And just where will you be while I'm hiding out in the john?"

A corner of Johannes's mouth twisted wryly. "You know me too well. I'll be working the crowd and the surrounding area trying to flush out the sniper. Ryan and Devon are coming up to help me. By the way, they're thrilled about your new mate. Kate's coming along with them. She wants to meet Audrey."

"Wonderful about Kate. Maybe she can field some of Audrey's questions." He blew out a tense breath. "I still don't like the idea of letting you fight my battles for me."

"Do you have a better idea?"

"Sure. I could show up. If they had a clear shot at me, you'd be sure to find them."

"Too risky."

"My reflexes saved me the last two times."

Johannes locked a hand around Max's forearm. "I don't care. We worked this out without your input because what you were doing couldn't be interrupted."

"Fine."

Johannes shot him a look. "You're a mated man now. Better learn the meaning of compromise."

"Isn't that when no one gets what they wanted?" Max made a sound between a snort and a grunt and then threw his hands in the air. "I can't stay mad at anyone today. We'll play it your way. I'll hide in a cupboard like an old woman and let you fight my battles."

"It's only one battle, Max. There are lots more coming. See you in the morning."

Max headed for the kitchen door. Before he got all the way through it, he turned. "Thanks for everything. You helped make tonight really special—for Audrey and me. I'll never forget it."

"You would've done the same for me. Give your mate a kiss and tell her it's from me."

~

Audrey floated up the stairs, drunk on love and sex. The reality of the huge house, fancy furniture, and food that didn't come via her wrist computer and ration coupons was all too much to wrap her mind around.

I'll just do this a step at a time.

She stopped to run her hands over a life-sized bronze statue of a medieval knight. It looked like an original piece and quite old. The workmanship was amazing. The knight had a hawk perched on one of his gauntlets. It looked so real, she imagined it taking flight and squawking as it flew around the open stairwell.

What to do about work? No way could she work for her husband, but since she'd already resigned, at least that wasn't a problem.

I guess I can go through with my plans. Since Max heads up the underground, I don't have to worry about finding them anymore.

She let herself into Max's bedroom—no, she corrected herself, it's our bedroom now—and flailed about finding the console panel that controlled the lights. Setting them on dim, she made her way to the bathroom and took a quick shower. Her pussy was sore, but it was a sweet ache. It reminded her how much she loved Max.

Audrey caught a glimpse of herself in the mirror that took up most of one wall. Three parallel lines scored her right side just over her ribs. Those must have been what burned like mad when she and Max were coupled in front of the fire. She fingered them softly. They were deep and would leave scars. "It's like I've been branded," she murmured and then smiled at her reflection, liking the concept.

She rummaged about until she found a toothbrush still encased in plastic and brushed her teeth. Further exploration yielded a hairbrush. Her locks were tangled; it took a few minutes to sort them out. Stumbling from weariness, she dimmed the bathroom lights and made her way to the bed. It smelled like sex and Max. Feeling silly, she pulled a pillow to her face and inhaled. Even though she didn't see how it could be possible after all the times she'd come, desire knifed through her.

Ach. My clothes. We'll have to get up at four, so I can go home and get more.

She tossed the bedclothes back and waved the lights up a notch. Audrey found her suit and blouse and stockings. Nothing was too badly wrinkled. Her panties had been ripped in two, but they weren't important. She giggled as she remembered Max destroying them and then got hangers from his closet. She hung her things with his, hoping his yummy, masculine scent would rub off on them, before retreating to the bed.

It was large and empty. She wanted to stay awake until Max came upstairs, but her eyes threatened to close. She must've fallen into a doze, because his voice jolted her awake.

"Ssht. Didn't want to wake you, love. Go back to sleep."

She burrowed into his embrace. "I didn't mean to fall asleep. My mind's racing a million miles an hour. So many things…"

"We don't have to solve any of them tonight." His deep voice rumbled against her hair.

"Probably not. We don't have to get up quite as early as I'd thought. I can wear the same things to the office tomorrow. Everything's intact but my panties."

"My ever-practical darling. So long as you're not dead to the world, I have good news. Kate and Devon will be here tomorrow. Along with Ryan."

"Wonderful. Tell me a little about them."

He cradled her against his body, an arm beneath her head. "Devon was a cop for the City of Berkeley. They hired him for one of the tracker task forces and gave him the serum."

"Let me guess," she murmured sleepily. "He shifted. They gave those guys way more than I took if what I read in the intel is right."

"Yes. He shifted. Before that, though, he'd been assigned to track Kate and bring her down. Problem was he was so taken by her, he couldn't bring himself to do anything other than follow her. She used to work as a sex surrogate and is quite attractive. He was so smitten, he even got a doctor's prescription to visit her. The way they explained it to me, he had his first shift while they were making love."

"How romantic."

"Not exactly. It scared the shit out of him. Kate said he took off out of her office like a bat out of Hell."

"But he came back."

Max nodded against the top of her head. "Yes. The mate bond can be pretty compelling. Anyway, they're happy for us, and I know Kate is excited to meet you. Ryan's done a whole lot of different things. In addition to a law enforcement background, he's also been a makeup artist. He's second in command for the underground's security force, which means he reports to Johannes."

She settled against him, feeling warm and cared for. Audrey thought about what Max had said about the other shifters' upcoming visit. An unpleasant premonition chilled her. "Is there a particular reason Ryan and Devon are coming?"

"Astute of you to ask. They think there will be another attempt on my life tomorrow at the press conference."

She wrenched out of his arms and sat bolt upright. "You're not going. You can't deliver yourself like a trussed pig."

He grunted. "Funny, Johannes said damn near the same thing. No, love, I'm not going. But we're not telling anyone that. We'll go out to lunch, and I'll develop a sudden case of stomach poisoning."

Relief whooshed through her. "Thank God. Our life together just began. I couldn't bear it if anything happened to you."

"Nothing's going to happen to me." He held out his arms. "Come here. We both need to get some sleep."

She lay back down. Fear beat an unpleasant tattoo in her mind. "Maybe it's not safe for you to serve the rest of your term."

"Maybe not. I assess things one day at a time. If I sent my worries spiraling too far ahead, I'd never accomplish anything."

"My dad used to say something like that."

"Do you know where he is?"

She shook her head. "No, but I'm pretty sure Loren does. Mom went into hiding with him. Couldn't bear to be parted, I guess. I'm the younger of their two kids. We didn't really need them anymore, but I still miss having a parent to talk with. Dad was really wise."

"Do you have any idea how old he is?"

"Not really. I did know he'd watch Mom grow old and die someday. He loved her beyond faith or reason. So much he didn't care she couldn't stand by his side throughout his life." Something warm cracked open inside Audrey. Tears spilled onto Max's chest. "I always hoped I'd find a love like that."

"And now you have." He kissed the top of her head and then her forehead.

"Daddy would really like you."

"I'm sure I'd like him too. Hopefully, we'll clean things up, so he and all the rest can finally come out of hiding."

CHAPTER 13

*I*t was closing on noontime when a stunning woman with long, curly red-blonde hair walked through the elevator on the arm of a dishy Native American man. She wore skin tight jeans and a multi-colored top that hugged considerable curves. Gold jewelry circled her neck and wrists. Her companion was dressed in black slacks, a pale green shirt, and a battered leather vest. His hair was drawn back in a braided queue. Behind them was another tall, rangy man, with straight red hair tumbling down his shoulders and multi-colored eyes, shading to gold. He wore tan khakis and a blue and green plaid flannel shirt.

"Hello." Audrey smiled. "Welcome to the Governor's office. How can I help you?"

"You must be Audrey." The woman grinned and strode forward. "I'm Kate Roman." She rounded Audrey's desk, pulled her to her feet, and hugged her. "I'm so happy for you," she whispered. "Max is just the best guy. We need to throw a party once this has all blown over."

"Thanks." Audrey extricated herself from Kate's embrace and gazed into dancing golden eyes. "From the sound of things, the celebration should be for you and Devon too."

"I want to meet Audrey." The Native American man stepped close and jostled Kate playfully.

Kate stepped aside. "Sorry. I'm hogging her. This is Devon."

"Pleased to meet you." The Indian man with arresting facial bone structure and liquid dark eyes held out a hand.

"I'm Ryan." The redhead shook her hand too.

"Max is expecting you. Will you be having lunch with us? I wasn't certain how many to make reservations for."

"It'll be all of us," Kate said. "Devon and I will spin a spot of magic like we always do out in public these days—to defeat all those APB posters." She shook her head in irritation. "Hope *that* blows over soon. Anyway, it's afterward that the boys have plans."

"Of course." Audrey eyed Devon and Ryan. She switched to mind speech a bit awkwardly. *"Take good care of him. Please."*

"We aim to," Ryan answered.

"If it's all the same to you," Devon cut in, "we'll push off now. If all goes as planned, we'll have time to visit over lunch and dinner."

"I'll look forward to it." Audrey watched as the men disappeared into the stairwell.

"So." Kate beamed. "We have a few minutes. Tell me everything."

Heat surged from Audrey's chest and swept over the top of her head. "But I barely know you," she protested.

Kate laughed, a warm, rich sound that put Audrey more at ease. "Don't mind me, hon. I worked as a surrogate for years. We don't pull any punches. I thrive on juicy, intimate details."

"Are you still working?"

"Oh my goodness, no. Once I met Devon, I knew I'd never make love with anybody else."

"With Devon, was it sort of instantaneous, like a bolt out of the blue?"

"Exactly." She switched to telepathic speech. *"It's the mate bond. It has such a strong draw, it's impossible to deny."*

Audrey inhaled deeply once and then again, feeling more comfortable. Kate was eminently likeable. Her bouncy effervescence was contagious. *"Even before the mate bond, I sort of worshipped Max from afar. Quite aside from being the most beautiful man I'd ever laid eyes on, he was kind and considerate, and I used to spin fantasies about dating him, once he wasn't governor anymore."*

Kate clapped her hands together. "Aw, I adore love stories. Even better, you had feelings for him and knew him quite well before. After all—" she lowered her voice conspiratorially "—secretaries know men much better than their wives. Just look at all the time you spent with him."

"Ready, ladies?" Max came through the stairwell door. He walked to Kate and kissed her cheek. "You're looking ravishing my dear, as always."

Kate quirked a brow and gestured toward Audrey, "What about your—?"

Audrey shook her head. "Uh-uh. His *secretary* is just fine."

"Sorry." Kate colored. "Wasn't thinking. This is a pretty public place."

"Car's waiting downstairs," Max said. "Loren will follow us, but we'll drive ourselves today."

～

THEY ATE at a little Mediterranean place not far from the office. After lunch, Max returned with Loren as planned. Audrey thought she'd be alone for a bit but welcomed Kate's company as she ferried the car to her midtown flat to retrieve enough clothes and personal effects to last a few days. Even though they'd only spent a couple of hours together, Kate already felt like an old friend.

Audrey parked as close to the door as she could and led Kate up the stairs to her apartment.

"I just love these old places," Kate trilled. "Berkeley is full of them. You'll have to come visit Devon and me. The cops ransacked my home, but we've got it looking decent again. We spent a lot of time at the shifter safe house while we were cleaning it up, and we're still there a few nights a week. Eventually we'll stay at my place full time. Thought it would be safer living there than at his house since I'm up in the hills—"

"How is it safe for you anywhere?" Audrey cut in, feeling worried for her new friend.

"We're pretty careful. Shifter magic is handy for shrouding your presence from others—so long as it isn't other shifters. They'd see through any illusion I could craft in about twelve seconds."

The door popped open before Audrey had a chance to retrieve her wrist computer from her suit jacket pocket and key in the code.

"Hey, we got lucky," a masculine voice boomed. Three men dove at her and Kate, grabbed their arms, and dragged them inside the apartment. Someone slammed the door.

"I'll say, two for the price of one."

"Hell of a bargaining chip."

Kate shrieked and clawed. Her clothes ripped as she shifted into a sleek mountain cat. The men had been ready for just such a move. All three of them dropped a net over her. The harder Kate clawed, the tighter the net clenched around her.

Fear turned Audrey's blood to ice. Her stomach curdled, and she wondered if she'd puke up her lunch. She would've made a dash for freedom. No one had actually harmed her yet, but she couldn't bring herself to leave Kate. Besides, she was pretty sure the second she cut and ran, one of the men would follow her. They were tall and heavily muscled; it looked like they spent a lot of time at a gym. If she made a break for it and one of them jumped her, he'd drive her face into the pavement outside. It wouldn't be pretty. Two of the men had short blond hair, the other dark, speckled with gray. Hard, flat, dark eyes stared at her.

"Let me out!" To Audrey's horror, her hands shimmered into paws with shiny, curved claws.

"Stop that! Shifting didn't work for Kate. They trapped her." Her hands stabilized in their human form. Audrey's wolf retreated, snarling imprecations at the men.

"How about it, sweetie," one of the men leered. "You gonna shift too?"

"I'm sure I have no idea what you're talking about."

"Like hell," a second man snorted.

The light flickered when Kate shifted. Human again, she was panting and disheveled.

"Let her go." Audrey was so intimidated, she could barely articulate the words. "She's naked."

"It's her own fucking fault," the man with dark hair said.

Audrey shoved her fear to a back burner and stormed up to him, hands on her hips. "It doesn't matter whose fault it is. There are three of you. It's not like we have any chance to escape. Let me take her into the bedroom and find something to cover her."

"I agree." One of the blonds said as he untangled his side of the webbing. "If someone saw us hauling a naked woman out of this building, they'd call the law." Kate snaked out a hand for her wrist computer, which had fallen onto the floor.

"I don't think so, darlin'." The blond man who'd spoken before snapped it up and pocketed it.

If anyone sees us leave here, I'll scream like a banshee.

Audrey helped Kate to her feet once the net had loosened enough to let her go. "Come on." She draped an arm around Kate's shoulders.

The men trooped after them.

Kate spun and sneered. "I don't need an audience."

"We've already seen everything, doll." A blond whistled appreciatively. "Besides, we know who you are—and what you used to do for a living. If you ever get tired of Devon, I could find a spot for you in my bed."

Kate spit at him. Her aim was good, and a glob of spittle hit his cheek.

"Bitch." He lunged forward, hand open to slap her.

"Stop." The dark haired man barked. "No damage unless it's absolutely necessary."

Humph. So they don't plan to hurt us.

Audrey's courage edged up a degree. She tugged open drawers and handed Kate a set of sweats and some panties.

"You should put on something more like this too," Kate murmured, getting into the offered clothing. "High heels and silk probably won't be very useful where they're taking us."

Audrey swallowed revulsion. She did not want to undress in front of the smirking group of men.

"Fine idea," one of the blond men chortled. "Love to see what this one's got."

"Yeah," the other blond muttered. "I've always been partial to strawberry blondes."

"Just go for it," Kate urged.

Teeth set together so hard they hurt, Audrey pulled another set of sweats from the drawer and some socks. She snagged tennis shoes from the closet and looked at Kate's bare feet.

"My shoes should be fine," Kate said, obviously reading Audrey's thoughts. "They're still on the floor in your front room."

Audrey turned her back to the men and took off her suit jacket and blouse. Kate handed her the sweat top and helped her get it over her head. Audrey kicked off her shoes and reached beneath her skirt to move her nylons out of the way. When her fingers touched nothing but bare skin, she remembered her lack of underwear and got another pair of panties from the drawer, pulling them on under her skirt once she'd gotten her panty hose off.

"Hey, doll," one of the men trilled. "You go bare bottom."

Someone whistled. She didn't know who since they were behind her.

"Yee-haw. My kind of woman."

"Shut the fuck up," she spat and tugged her sweat bottoms on beneath her skirt. Once she was covered, she undid the skirt and slid it to the floor.

"Not much of a show," one of the men complained.

"More than you deserved," Kate growled. "Here, hon." She

handed Audrey's shoes and socks to her. "I'm going to go find mine. Thanks for the clothes."

"No problem." Audrey sat on the edge of the bed and put on her shoes and socks. Her wrist computer was in a pocket of her suit jacket. *Damn!* She wished she'd thought of it before she'd agreed to change clothes. Maybe there'd be a way she could rescue it and slip it beneath her sweats. She got up and went to her clothing piled on the floor. Thank God, she always kept the wrist computer on silent mode.

"What are you doing?" the dark-haired man asked, his voice sharp. The others had followed Kate to the living room.

She smiled sweetly. "Hanging them up. My work clothes cost a fortune. So does dry cleaning."

He rolled his eyes. "You're making a whole lot of assumptions. Like that you'll ever see the inside of this place again. Be quick about it."

She draped everything over her arm and walked briskly to the closet. Using her body as a shield, she hung things, taking her time arranging them.

"Tom," one of the men called from the living room.

"Yeah."

Audrey took advantage of what she hoped was a moment of inattention to slide the computer out of the suit pocket and into one she'd sewn into her sweat pants for just that purpose. She held her breath. Adrenaline coursed, making her scalp tingle unpleasantly.

"We need to get out of here," the living room voice continued.

"Hey." Tom clumped to her and grabbed her arm. "We're leaving. You did a good enough job."

"Okay. Okay." Exultant she'd pulled it off, Audrey went with him. Now if she could just grab a second alone to use the computer, maybe she could call in the cavalry to free them.

"No funny stuff." One of the blonds brandished a laser pistol. The men herded them through the door. Blondie number two took off down the stairs.

"I heard you say you weren't supposed to hurt us," Kate said, her chin high.

Tom grinned nastily. "That's not to say one of you might not meet with an unpleasant accident."

"All clear. Come now," floated up to them.

There wasn't a soul in sight when the men prodded her and Kate into the back of a large luxury car. "It's just like mine." Kate's gaze roamed the inside of the vehicle. "Not many people kept these older ones."

One of the blonds sat in the back seat with them next to a door, presumably to block one of the sources of egress. The car took off at a sedate pace. Audrey tried to see what the dark-haired man tapped into the onboard nav system, but he shielded his activity with a hand.

She squeezed her eyes shut. Max would be frantic when he didn't hear from her. She was supposed to pick up a few clothes, drop them at his house, and come back to the office.

One thing at a time. If I get too far ahead of myself, I'll be so scared I won't be able to do anything.

She smiled grimly. Max had said something very similar the previous night, leaving out the scared part. She suspected very little frightened him.

"So." She straightened in her seat. "I know Tom's name. Who are the rest of you?"

"It's not important," Tom snapped in a tone that made it clear he was furious one of the others had used his name.

"Why, of course it is," Kate drawled. "I'd love to get to know you boys better."

"Huh? You had a change of heart after you tried to scratch our eyes out?" Tom turned to stare at her from his place behind the wheel.

"Hey, honey. I worked as a surrogate for years. You know how we are. We need to get laid—often and regularly. It's why we pick that line of work. You're all pretty good looking specimens. But I like to know men's names before I fuck them."

Tom's face reddened; he turned back around. Despite his bold talk in her apartment, Audrey was certain he hadn't had much experience with women. "Well," he mumbled, "you already know mine."

"She's working us," back seat blond snarled. "This one's a hot mamma. We know all about her."

Kate batted her eyes at him. She shimmied across the seat and laid a hand over his crotch. "Want to try me, big guy? Oh, Audrey. This one's hung. Maybe we could share him."

Audrey played along. "Sounds like a plan." She scooted closer. "Let me feel too."

Back seat blond turned beet red. He slapped Kate's hand away. "I like my sex private," he growled.

"Well," Kate's golden gaze bored into his dark eyes. "Looks like you'll know right where to find me."

They drove for a long time. Audrey recognized the expressway and understood they were heading for the Bay Area. She wondered why their captors hadn't blindfolded them. And then she figured it out. These guys were rank amateurs. They didn't do this sort of thing often. In fact, maybe they'd never done anything like it before.

"Hey." She tried mind speech with Kate.

The other woman sidled close, jabbed her, and shook her head almost imperceptibly. A conversation with Max roared to life in Audrey's head. The three men in the car had to be shifters. It made sense because that was who was after him. Kate somehow knew it, which was why she'd vetoed telepathic speech. The men would be able to hear them, at least as long as they were all together in this car.

Audrey let her head rest against the softly padded seats. She couldn't do anything right now. The car's doors were locked when it was in motion.

I just have to bide my time. We'll find a way out of this.

She considered talking with her wolf, but if the men could hear a conversation with Kate, maybe they could hear one with the wolf too.

Christ, but I wish I knew more about being a shifter. I don't know squat.

She reached for Kate's hand where it sat between their bodies and squeezed it. The answering pressure from Kate heartened her. It was selfish, but Audrey was glad the other woman was there. Being alone with these men, shifters who would stop at nothing to bring Max down, would've paralyzed her.

Guess that old saying about strength in numbers is truer than I ever could have guessed.

CHAPTER 14

Max paced up and down the great room inside his mansion. Devon did the same. When Audrey and Kate failed to return to the office and didn't answer pages on their wrist computers, Max had texted Johannes, Ryan, and Devon. The men had raced to Max's office. Despite frantic efforts, they hadn't found any clues at the Capitol Rotunda, snooping around the cancelled news conference. Because Max and Devon were wild with worry and fear for their mates, the other two men had hustled them down the elevator and driven to Max's.

An hour had dribbled past since then.

Ryan and Johannes worked the vid feed with a fury, trying to nail down clues. Max had gone from wolf to human so many times, he'd lost track of what he was now. He opened his mouth to howl; a guttural shriek filled the air.

Hands shook his shoulders. "Goddammit. Stand still," Johannes shouted. "We need to talk with you. Devon, you knock it off too."

"I'm going to kill those bastards who nabbed Kate." Devon slammed a ham-sized fist into a delicate side table. It crumpled beneath the assault. "Shit! Sorry. I'll replace it."

"Not possible," Max snapped. "It was built in the sixteen

hundreds. The table doesn't matter. What does is finding out who took the women. And where they are. I've tried to raise Audrey through our mate bond, but I can't, which means she's several miles away." He glanced at the scraps that had been his clothes. "I'm going to find pants and a shirt. Want me to hunt you down something too?" he asked Devon.

"I don't care. I suppose I'll need clothes before we leave here. I tried Kate through the mate bond too. No dice."

His pale green, long-sleeved T-shirt and black jeans lay in a shredded mess on the Oriental rug. He'd shifted nearly as many times as Max, ripping a line of stitches from a recent injury, sustained fighting his way out of the Berkeley Police Station with the rest of the tracker task force.

All of them had rebelled against their bosses, going rogue. The ones who'd been turned into full-blown shifters by the serum were furious the brass held their new status against them. After all, they'd had to accept the IV infusions or get fired. The few human members of the task force had supported the shifters in a show of solidarity.

"Mine will fit better," Johannes said, his hazel eyes pinched with compassion. "Do you want them now or later?"

"Now. Once I know whatever you found out, I'm out of here. Goddamn motherfucking sonofabitch." Devon slammed his forehead with the heel of one hand. "I can't believe they've got my Kate."

"Someone's going to pay," Max growled. "If they've harmed so much as one of Audrey's hairs, they're dead meat."

"Let's all shift. We can run as a pack and track them down," Max's wolf snarled.

"We need to find out where they are, first," Max explained. *"If they're a long way from here, we'll need to drive—or fly."*

"I listened in," Devon said unapologetically. "My mountain cat said the same thing. Do you have a hovercraft big enough for all four of us?"

Max nodded. His gaze raked over Johannes and Ryan. Fury burned a hole inside his chest. "Did you locate them?"

"We think so. Go get something on."

Max raced up the stairs, taking them three at a time. He trusted Johannes would find something for Devon—and patch up his trashed stitches. Feeling crazed, head about to explode from tension, Max pulled on black sweat pants, a black turtleneck, and a black jacket followed by black boots. He found black gloves and a black watch cap to hide his fair hair. Ryan had been a makeup artist before the shit had hit the fan. He could black out their faces. He never went anywhere without his kit.

In less than five minutes, Max strode back into the front room. Johannes was dressing Devon's side with fresh gauze squares. Though his torso was bare, he had on black jeans. The expression on his face broke Max's heart. He knew how much Kate meant to the Native American man because he was just as frantic about Audrey.

"Report," he barked at Ryan. "Do that grease paint thing on my face while you're talking."

A corner of Ryan's mouth twisted. "Somehow, I anticipated you'd want to take advantage of my other skill set." He picked up a clear vinyl case from the floor, set it on a chair, and opened it, withdrawing brushes and small pots.

"Talk."

"Damn straight," Devon cut in.

"We hacked into their network," Johannes said, straightening from his work on Devon's side. "It was easy, and the kidnapping is all over it. The shifter group that took Audrey and Kate has their base of operations in Tiburon."

"Is that where they've taken Kate?" Devon interrupted. He tugged a dark gray sweater over his head and buckled his shoulder holster into place.

"We're not sure—" Ryan began.

"What do you mean you're not sure? What the fuck good is that going to do?" Max shouted. He dropped into a chair and rubbed his forehead with his fingertips. "I'm sorry. I'll shut up."

"Their proposed destination wasn't on the vid feed," Johannes clarified.

"We think they'd be stupid to bring the women to their headquarters," Ryan hurried on.

"Yes," Johannes said. "We believe they're taking them to the Bay Area somewhere but probably not into their operations center."

"Is there a way to track them?" Max asked, fighting for some level of rational thought.

"We don't know." Ryan's voice was flat. He smeared makeup on Max's face. "Because we need to leave this house to try."

"Yes!" Devon leapt to his feet. "We'll start with Audrey's place. It was where the women were going."

"We could've done that an hour ago if the two of you hadn't been so rabid," Johannes muttered. "Put some of that crap on my face, Ryan."

"Don't know that I need it," Devon said. "My skin's pretty dark."

Ryan glanced his way. "You do. It only takes a second."

"I'll get us some firepower." Max loped to the far side of the room and clicked the display of his wrist computer. A section of wall slid aside. He grabbed a laser pistol for himself and another for Johannes. Max half turned. "Ryan?"

The shifter snorted. "You're kidding. I've got my own. What kind of security deputy would I be if I had to borrow a gun?"

Max pushed a recessed button, and the wall moved back into place.

"Let's take the hovercraft to Audrey's," Devon suggested. "We can leave from there with whatever we find."

Max shook his head. "Uh-uh. There's still the rule about no hovercraft within the city limits."

"But you're the governor," Devon protested. "That gives you privileges."

Max squeezed his eyes shut. They felt hot and gritty. He opened them and looked from one man to the next. "Yes, it gives me privileges. I also do not want our whereabouts broadcasted. I don't want anyone following us or wondering what the fuck we're doing."

"All right." Devon balled his hands into fists. "What do you propose?"

"We'll take one of the cars to Audrey's and find out what we can. I'll collect my car. It has to be there."

"No it doesn't," Ryan broke in. "The kidnappers might have shanghaied it."

"I don't think so," Max said. "We probably won't be that lucky. Taking my car would've been incredibly short-sighted. It has a tracking device, so the cops always know where it is."

"Go on." Devon pounded a fist into his open palm and shifted from foot to foot. The need to get moving poured off him.

"We'll return here. By then it will be dark. We'll leave without filing a flight plan and without electronics, so it will be harder to track us."

"I hope to God we have a solid destination by then." Johannes's voice was so low, it took Max's lupine senses to hear him.

You and me both.

"Come on," Max said. "Let's roll."

Audrey sat on a chilly concrete floor in what looked like a bunker left over from times when Americans were scared shitless the Russians were going to bomb them. The eight by ten windowless room was dimly lit by a single bulb hanging from the ceiling. A bucket sat in one corner: her toilet. Other than the bucket, the room was empty. She had no idea where the men had taken Kate.

She scanned the small space again, then got to her feet and walked the length of each wall, hunting for cameras or any electronic surveillance equipment. She wanted to try her wrist computer—but not if someone was watching her. Finally, she huddled in a corner. With her body as a barrier, she dragged the computer out of its pocket, powered it up, and glanced at the signal strength. Zero bars.

I must be underground. A long way underground.

She hung her head and gritted her teeth together to manage crushing disappointment. She'd been so hopeful. A tear slid down one cheek. She secreted the computer back in its place in her pants and continued her circuit of the room. If anyone was watching, perhaps they wouldn't think anything of her stint in the corner. After all, she wasn't there very long.

A faint scratching came from behind her. Audrey cocked her head and dialed in her lupine senses to listen.

At least I can do that much with my neophyte shifter skills.

Yes, she hadn't imagined it. There it was again. She moved to where the sound was loudest and sat on the floor so she could make a scratching noise back.

Soon, a pattern emerged. Eleven scratches, a pause, one scratch, a pause…

Kate.

Her friend was spelling out things with scratches. Audrey scratched *I understand* back. It took forever to communicate, but both women hadn't been harmed—not yet anyway.

According to Kate, if they'd had a private moment apart from their shifter guards, they should've been able to reach their men through the mate bond. Unfortunately, that gift only extended for about ten miles. Once they left the capital area, that possibility vanished right along with them.

The back and forth messaging was laborious and time-consuming, but it took her mind off the desperate nature of her situation. No one knew their location. They were at the mercy of an insane group of shifters who wanted Max dead and the shifter underground disbanded.

She managed to ask Kate about talking to her wolf. Kate scratched back, *don't, they'll intercept it.* They were in the middle of a conversation about escape ideas when her door clicked open.

Tom stood framed in the doorway. "Get up. You're coming with me."

Audrey scrambled to her feet. Terror thickened her throat and burned in her stomach. What were they going to do to her? Would they torture her? "I-I don't know anything," she stammered.

"Get moving. I'll drag you if I have to."

Maybe he'll take me higher where I can use the computer.

Audrey hung onto that thought. Hope was all she had. Without it, she'd sink into a writhing mass of hysterical nerves. They walked to the end of a hallway lined with the same concrete blocks that had formed the walls of her cell. Tom passed his hand over an electronic plate. A door whirred open, and she stepped into an elevator that whisked them upward.

"How deep were we?" she asked, trying to keep her voice from shaking.

"Doesn't matter. We ask the questions around here."

She raised her chin. "Too bad. My next one was where are you taking me?"

He didn't answer. She tried another gambit. Maybe if she could shock him, or piss him off, he'd spill something important she could use to escape. "I know you're a shifter."

He rounded on her, dark eyes on fire. "You damn betcha. A real one. Not some phony whore like you. Fucking serum. Made a whole bunch of you into what you should never have been."

Anger kindled. It felt good and gave her courage. "Really? Your priorities are skewed. You need every single one of us to throw off the government's yoke. I'd think you'd be grateful. I took a hell of a chance with the black market. I could have poisoned myself."

"Too bad you didn't."

"Never mind I just outed myself, how could you tell about me taking the serum?"

"I sense how much shifter blood you have. It shouldn't be

enough for you to shift, but I saw a paw form back in your apartment." He shrugged. "Doesn't take a quantum leap to assume you injected yourself."

The elevator door opened. He shoved her through so roughly, she nearly tumbled headlong. "Let me tell you something, sister. Being a shifter is a God-given gift. When you manipulate it with science, you cheapen it. If you'd been meant to be born one of us, you would've been. March." He pointed down a long hall. This one had sheetrock walls, and light spilled through the occasional window.

We're above-ground. Now if I can just get a moment to myself. "Uh, is there a bathroom?"

"You had a bucket in your cell."

"I was just thinking about using it when you showed up."

His face twisted into a grimace, and he clicked his wrist computer. A stone-faced woman with short black hair and blue eyes emerged through a door and grabbed her wrist. "I'll take you. No funny business." She flashed a laser pistol and then tucked it back under her jacket.

The woman pushed open a door on the opposite side of the hall. Audrey's heart squeezed. No stalls. Just a toilet in one corner and a sink. Heat rose to her face. "Are you going to watch me?"

"Yes. If you really have to go. Get it over with."

Audrey sat and peed, careful to cover the computer's bulge in her pocket with a hand. "Thanks." She tried a smile once she was done, but the woman just grunted, opened the door, and turned her back over to Tom.

Questions rumbled through Audrey's head. She'd gotten Tom talking before when she'd asked if he were a shifter. "So—" she aimed for a neutral tone "—why aren't you blaming the government for the edict that drove you into hiding?"

"What's the point? Things weren't all that bad. A lot of us were still working under the table, and the black market had everything we needed." He blew out an angry-sounding breath. "The underground blew things all to hell."

"How?" Despite being a prisoner and at the splinter group's mercy, she was curious.

"You'll be questioned inside the council chamber. Ask them."

"Do you think they'll answer me?"

He shrugged. "Who the fuck knows? Stop here." He placed his palm on another glass plate. A double door popped open, and he shoved her inside.

Throat so tight it was hard to get a full breath, Audrey looked around her. She was in a large room. Tan walls, with peeling paint, and a scarred linoleum floor suggested no one bothered with maintenance. Windows looked out on other buildings. She knew they were somewhere in the North Bay, but her abductors had finally gotten around to blindfolding both her and Kate half an hour before the car quit moving.

A raised dais spanned one side of the room. Four men sat in chairs and stared at her. Two were older with long, graying hair. The other two didn't look a day over thirty. One was the back seat blond from their drive to the North Bay. The other had short, light brown hair, and Audrey didn't recognize him. Maybe twenty-five other people sat in folding chairs scattered at random around the room. Everyone was dressed in ragged clothing with multiple patches.

Compassion cut through her fear. These were her people. Look what had happened to them. "I'm sorry," she murmured.

"You'll be a whole lot sorrier before we're done with you, sister," one of the older men at the front of the room said. "Hook her up."

"Hook me up to what?"

"You talk too much." Tom closed a hand over her upper arm and dragged her to a wall outfitted with large eye-bolts and leather straps. "Take off your top."

"No." Audrey closed her arms over her chest. Two men rose

from nearby chairs. They each grabbed an arm. While they held her arms over her head, Tom pulled her top off.

"When you feel the whip, you won't be saying no," one observed before returning to his chair.

"*Let me out. Now.*" Claws pressed against her fingertips. One protruded.

She considered taking a swipe at Tom, but the whole room would mob her if she hurt one of theirs.

"*I know you want to do something, but I can't see where being a wolf would help us right now.*" The claw retracted.

Tom eyed her oddly. "Smart move, missy. Turn around and face the wall."

"I'm not going to try to escape. That would be stupid." Audrey aimed her words at the four men on the dais. "Can't we just talk?"

"Oh, we'll talk all right," one of the gray-haired men snapped. "First, you'll be punished."

"For what?"

"Taking a drug to force your body to shift."

Tom grabbed her shoulders and spun her to face the wall, slamming her body into it. Pain ratcheted through her. He held her against the wall with the length of his powerful body while he buckled the leather straps around her wrists.

Conversation ebbed and flowed around her. No one lifted so much as a finger to help. They talked about how soon the punishment would begin. Annoyance that *not everyone is here yet*, was a common theme.

I'm trapped in a bad science fiction movie.

Tom's weight moved off her. She tugged both wrists, but the leather only tightened. Her arms ached already. She could imagine how they'd feel if these barbarians left her like this for very long.

"How many?" a voice called.

"Twenty lashes."

"What is this?" Audrey craned her head around and tried to look at the four men. "The Middle Ages? Flogging went out hundreds of years ago."

"Aye, Miss," a voice with a strong Scottish burr said. "There are those of us who are that old—and older. We remember how effective it can be." A high-pitched whistling sound filled the air just before liquid fire exploded the length of her back.

"Stop! No more! Stop! Stop!" Audrey screamed and screamed again. She'd never experienced pain so searing. The whip fell again. And again. After six strokes, she wished for unconsciousness. After ten, she hoped she'd die. Blood dripped down her back and spattered the floor.

"Are you going to let them kill us without putting up a fight?" her wolf demanded.

"Yes. No. I don't know. I can't think anymore. Hurts too bad."

"Pull your head out of your ass, and stop feeling sorry for yourself. You cannot die in human form. It will doom me to a half-life."

Her wolf's words sank through the pain-haze, and she shook herself. *"Sorry. I didn't know. I'm ready to shift if you are. Maybe we can take out a few of these bastards before they kill us."*

The whip landed again. The raw sounds emerging from her throat gave her energy. She'd fight back, goddammit.

"This will take both of us," the wolf cautioned. *"Reach for my form on my count of three."*

"Got it," she gritted through clenched teeth. *"Let's do this."*

"What the fuck are you doing?" a voice rang out from behind her. There was something familiar about it, but Audrey couldn't figure it out. Footsteps pounded toward her, and then arms closed around her body.

His scent and his voice clicked. Relief made her light-headed. "Daddy?"

"Yes, princess. No one's going to hurt you anymore. I'll get you down."

CHAPTER 15

*R*on Westen undid her wrists and cradled her against him. The material of his corduroy shirt felt soft and soothing next to her face. Audrey was beyond tears. Her back hurt so much, even thinking took a huge effort.

"We weren't done," a voice from the front of the room cracked like the whip that had done so much damage.

"Too fucking bad. This is my daughter. You will not hurt her further. Send someone with a first aid kit over here." Every inch of Ron's six-foot-four frame quivered. He'd kept himself in superb shape, and his blond hair only had a touch of gray in it. Blue eyes kindled with outrage as he silently dared the others to countermand him.

"You don't issue orders, Westen."

"Today I do." He kissed Audrey's forehead and took her to a chair. "I'm so sorry, princess. If I'd known one of the captives was you, I'd have been here on time. None of this would've happened."

Audrey raised her tear-streaked face. "Is this—" she waved a hand weakly in the air "—common enough you all just accept it? You said *captives* as if you've seen a lot of them."

Her father dropped his gaze, looking ashamed. A woman walked over carrying a red box with a white cross on it. Audrey clamped her jaws together and struggled to her feet. She pointed at the first aid kit. "That can wait. This can't. You all know I work for Maximillian Sigayev, Governor of California and head of the shifter underground. It's why you kidnapped me. What you probably don't know is I'm also his mate."

Whispers with an angry undercurrent spread through the room. Audrey ignored them. "Kate, the other woman you snapped up, was just collateral damage. She's a bona fide shifter and from everything I've heard a damned brave one. You should run down, free her, and beg her forgiveness."

A rustle ran through the crowd. Audrey sucked in a deep breath. As long as she stood still, her injuries were manageable.

"You do not have the floor," back seat blond thundered. He jumped to his feet and brandished a fist.

"I can't believe Max would mate with a half breed," someone cried out.

Audrey turned toward the voice. "Oh, really?" she mocked. "You hate him so much you kidnapped me to get to him, and now you're worried about who he takes as his mate? How touching." She held up her right hand, so the mating wound was visible. "I'm many things, but not a liar. The cuts on my side from the ritual mating stone have probably been obliterated by the whip marks."

"You've been told you do not have the floor. Sit down," one of the gray-haired men at the front table shouted.

"I'm not ceding my right to speak," Audrey shouted back. "You have nothing to lose by listening to me. I have much more timely intel than you because I've been living in the world you ran away from."

An ugly sound moved through the throng. Audrey jumped on it. "Yes, ran away and left your fellow shifters to fend for themselves. Things weren't going all that well—for any of you—and then the government developed that serum you all think is demon-spawned."

She moved closer to the dais. "It's not. It's your salvation." She held her hands out in front of her. "Don't you see? It's what will create enough of you to get the edict repealed once and for all. Even politicians, as self-serving and dimwitted as they are, understand they can't wage a war against half their constituency.

"I asked for the serum, goddammit. Of my own free will. I put myself at risk getting it from the black market. It might not have been pure. It could have been poison. It might have killed me." Audrey pounded a fist into her thigh and winced as the movement set her flayed skin on fire. "I did it for you. For all of us. So we could walk free with our heads high again."

"So now you're some sort of Joan of Arc," back seat blond sneered.

"No, I'm a shifter just like you." Audrey paused to let her words sink in and then repeated them. "Yes, just like you. If I weren't, Max couldn't have formed a mate bond with me." She waved her hands expansively in front of her despite waves of pain in her back. "Just look at yourselves. Your clothes are rags. This room hasn't seen paint or even simple cleaning in a long time. This isn't living. You're surviving. Where's your pride, goddammit? At least if you were part of the underground, you'd have jobs and meaning in your lives other than waiting out the Gotterdammerung."

"Audrey, princess, come sit down." Her father moved to her side. "You're overwrought."

She turned to him. "Yes, I am. With good reason. Abraham Lincoln said, *A house divided against itself cannot stand.* We're not any different. We have to work together." Audrey turned back to the group in front of the room and lowered her voice. She'd been practically screaming. "You did what you thought best at the time. I understand that because my father is one of the most level-headed men I've ever known, and he took my mother, the love of his life, and joined you in hiding."

Ron snorted. "Your mother insisted on coming with me. Wouldn't take *no* for an answer."

Someone in the crowd chuckled. It was contagious. The mood in the room split wide open with everyone talking at once. Audrey squeezed her eyes shut and sagged against her father, taking care to lean on her shoulder.

"Thank God. They're going to listen to reason."

"I hope so." Ron spoke right into her ear. "It's why I was late. I can't stand these public floggings. I've been trying to talk sense into this group for a long time. Even though I haven't heard the term in a long time, *Gotterdammerung* was right on. We've become the authors of our own destruction."

The doors at the back of the room slammed against their stops. Max raced into the room with Devon, Johannes, and Ryan right behind him. All the men had their guns drawn. "Jesus Christ! Audrey." Max raced to her side and slammed a fist into Ron's side. "Leave her alone, you bastard. She's my mate."

"Max!" Audrey jumped between him and her father, her back screaming in protest. "That's my father. He saved me."

"Then why does your back look like you just came off a public flogging block?" Max's gaze radiated anguish as he pulled Audrey gently against him.

"Because I didn't get here in time." Ron held out a hand. "I'm sorry, and I'm glad to meet Audrey's mate." A corner of his mouth turned down. "Never could stand her first husband."

"Where is my mate?" Devon thundered. He stood in front of the dais, laser pistol leveled at the four men.

"She's fine," back seat blond said.

"Yes, put that away before it goes off by accident," one of the gray-haired men said.

Devon made no move to holster his weapon. "It would serve you right if it did. Where is she?" His features curled into a grimace, teeth bared. Audrey could almost see his mountain lion self just beneath the surface.

"In some sort of dungeon way underground," Audrey said. "There's an elevator."

"I'll show you," Ron volunteered and headed out the door.

"Come back after you lead him to Kate," Audrey called after him. "I need to hear how Mom is."

"Don't worry, princess. I'm done being separated from my family." He and Devon disappeared into the hall.

Max wrapped his arms around her. Audrey shrieked.

"Sorry, sorry. Is there a fucking first aid kit anywhere? Johannes, get over here."

Johannes trotted toward them, grabbing the first aid supplies from the woman on his way. He eyed Audrey's back and whistled. "Holy crap! You may need stitches." He rustled through the kit. "This is going to sting like a bitch. Max, hang onto her."

Sting was a mild term. Her back flared into agony. "Arrrrgh. What are you doing?" she shrieked.

"Sluicing the cuts with iodine and alcohol. In the old days, we would've used whiskey. It should be easing off."

Audrey sucked in a shaky breath. "It is."

"We'll get you to a doctor just as soon as we leave here," Max promised, his face a study in torment. "Audrey, my mate, my love. When I knew you'd been taken, I almost couldn't live with myself. I failed you. I should have been by your side."

She leaned against his chest. "Don't be ridiculous. You had no way of knowing. None of us did. I don't know if I'll be able to stand fabric against my skin, but I'd like to put my top back on."

"Where is it?" Max asked. She pointed.

"I'll get it," Ryan said.

Max's ice-blue gaze swept the room, and he set his jaw in a determined line. "You, all of you, are my people. We're all shifters. We must stand as a unit. If we do, we'll win."

"Your mate made that abundantly clear before you got here," the man on the dais with light brown hair said. "She's a hell of an ambassador. I can't speak for the others, but I'm ready to talk with you."

"I'm not sure I am," the gray-haired man who'd ordered her to sit said.

"Why not, Igor?" Max demanded. "I've known you all my life. You were part of my family pack back in Russia. You're practically a blood relation. Why don't you trust me?"

Igor drew his thick, gray brows together. "I have not forgotten. I thought you had."

Max shook his head. "We never forget. It's one of the blessings of our long lives. I saved your sister from her warlock husband who forced her to remain in her wolf form and do perverse things with him."

"Do you know all these people?" Audrey interrupted, surprise running through her. Were all shifters so interconnected they knew one another's family histories?

Max turned to her. "Most of them, although I'd never met your father before."

She straightened, extricating herself from his arms, and faced the room full of shifters. "If you know Max, how could any of you have ever doubted him? I've only worked with him for a year-and-a-half and even I, half-breed shifter that you've labeled me, recognize he's the most honorable man I've ever met. You should be ashamed of yourselves."

"Enough." The first gray-haired man held up both hands. "We're ready to see what you have to offer." A susurrus of assent rose from many mouths.

"Nice work, Audrey. Ever considered a career in politics?" Max beamed at her before turning to the four on the dais. "It's about time. If you joined the underground, we'd be unbeatable. You and all the other splinter groups."

Igor cracked half a grin. "Son, I'm almost starting to believe you."

Max quirked a brow. "Golden-tongued politician that I am, you'd best listen carefully. I might try to sell you a boatload of shit."

The room erupted in laughter just as Kate and Devon swept into the room arm in arm with Ron right behind them.

~

AUDREY SNUGGLED NEXT TO MAX. Johannes had taped gauze over her wounds and wrapped a large elastic bandage loosely over everything. It compressed her breasts, but the relief it gave her back was a good tradeoff for the mild discomfort. She and Kate spent hours listening while the men hammered out negotiations. Kate had jumped into the fray frequently, but Audrey honestly didn't feel she knew enough to contribute anything significant, as many of the fine points they argued over didn't mean anything to her.

"Ready to go, love?" Max asked. "You look exhausted. I still think we need to get medical attention for your back. I can have one of our shifter docs stop by once we're home."

"Not quite." Audrey got to her feet and walked to where her father sat. "I didn't follow everything you talked about, but the gist of part of it was you and Mom are rejoining the land of the living."

Ron smiled at her. "That's right, princess. If your mother doesn't shoot me for not bringing you home to see her as long as you were so close."

Audrey bit her lip. An idea bubbled to the surface, but she hesitated. In any other situation, she would've held a private conversation with Max first, but she swallowed hard and said, "Max, would it be all right if my mom and dad stayed with us? Just until they can find housing."

"Darling." Max joined her and dropped a hand on Ron's shoulder. "Of course they can. The house is so large, most of it never gets used."

"You don't have to—" Ron began.

"I know that," Max cut in. "We want to. Audrey's been by herself for far too long."

"We'd pay you rent."

Max rolled his eyes. "We'll talk about it."

"No. I insist, or we'll come up with something else."

"See." Audrey's eyes gleamed with sudden tears. "I come by my stubborn streak honestly."

"The address is four-fifty-seven..." Max rattled off the rest.

"Whenever you arrive is fine. Text Audrey so we can make certain someone is home."

"I'd hug you," Ron grinned at her, "but I think I should wait until your back heals."

"Thanks, Dad." Audrey kissed his forehead and straightened. "Now I'm ready," she told Max.

The four men and two women were a tight fit in the hovercraft. Max joked about it being so heavy it wouldn't fly, but somehow it gained altitude and headed for Sacramento.

"How'd you find us?" Kate asked.

"It's a long story," Devon said. The arm that hadn't left his mate's side tightened around her when he pulled her against him.

"I hate to admit it," Johannes smirked, "but we got lucky."

"I prefer to call it well-honed hunches and skill," Ryan cut in smoothly.

"How about if one of you starts at the beginning and the other three keep quiet," Audrey suggested.

"Bully idea," Kate seconded.

"We started on the vid feed," Max said. "Ryan and Johannes gathered everything they could while Devon and I acted like testosterone-laden asses tearing up and down the living room."

Audrey stifled a giggle. She could just picture the two of them. "It feels mighty good to be cared about that much."

"Excellent," Max said gruffly. "Because you are. Anyway, we discovered who'd taken you but not where. So we went to your apartment. Found my car there. It had been stripped."

A hand flew to Kate's mouth. "Oh my God. Sorry."

"It doesn't make any difference. Besides, what were the two of you going to do? Say 'No, we can't leave, we have to guard Max's car.'?"

Kate chuckled. "Well, when you put it like that…"

"The women asked us not to interrupt," Johannes said.

"Glad you pointed that out." Ryan snickered. "All they've done is interrupt since Max started talking."

"We'll be good," Kate said.

"Promise," Audrey added.

Max cleared his throat. "Once we got to Audrey's, Devon nosed around. He's really, really good at trolling for clues. He found a bunch of hairs that obviously didn't belong to Audrey."

"It wasn't a bunch. I found three. Damned lucky to stumble across them. I combed the rug with a magnifying glass." Devon shot Audrey a meaningful look. "Good thing you didn't have a dog or cat."

Audrey furled a brow. "Guess it's good I only shifted once there. I'm sure my wolf sheds."

"Why wouldn't I?" she inquired archly.

"I was wondering what happened to you, sweetie. You've been awfully quiet."

"It's because we were hurt. You won't be able to shift until you heal up some."

"Aw." Audrey sent loving feelings inward. *"The wait will be just as hard for me."*

"Thank you."

"No, thank you for being my wolf."

Kate creased her forehead in thought. "The kidnappers might have lost a hair or two when I shifted and tried to take them on—before they dropped that fucking net over me."

"Good thing you did that." Devon kissed her. "In any event, I had Johannes ferry the hairs to the Sac City Police and called in a favor or two. Hair has good DNA tracings. We ID'd two of the men who kidnapped you. By then it was getting dark. We flew to Tiburon, scared the crap out of their wives, and found out where they were holding you."

"The whole thing took way longer than I would've liked," Max said. "Hang on, we're home. It's going to be a rough landing because we're so heavy." The craft thudded against the hovercraft landing pad next to the house.

"Not so bad," Kate said. "I've had worse."

Max powered the craft down. "We can talk more over breakfast. I'm taking Audrey to our room. If it wasn't the middle of the night, I'd get a doctor in. Do we have any antibiotics, Johannes?"

"Yes. I'll drop them in front of your door, along with a glass of milk and some crackers. They'll sit better if her stomach's not empty."

Audrey walked into the house clinging to Max's arm. Her back ached, and she was so tired she thought she might sleep the clock round.

"Do you want anything from downstairs?" Max asked.

"Whiskey."

He laughed. "Not a good idea. Booze and antibiotics don't mix well. I'll bet I can find some pain pills, though."

"Maybe some crackers and cheese or something. I haven't eaten since lunch yesterday. Oh, that's right. Johannes said he'd leave crackers and milk or something along with antibiotics."

"I'll see you up the stairs, and then I'll come back down and get a tray together. We can do better than crackers and milk."

"For Pete's sake, I'm not an invalid. I'll find my own way to our room."

"Are you sure?"

She nodded. "I really like it when you try to take care of me, though. Don't stop."

"Don't worry. It's hardwired in. You're my mate. When I thought you were lost to me, I tore the living room apart." He shook his head. "I'll see what can be salvaged tomorrow."

"I love you, Max." She turned to face him and stood on tiptoes to brush her lips against his.

"I want to crush you against my body and never, never let you go." His voice held a low, urgent note. "But I'd hurt you if I did that. I love you more than my life. Nothing bad will ever happen to you again. I swear it."

"Hey!" Johannes chugged by them. "Watch her back."

"I plan to watch all of Audrey," Max retorted. "Thanks for getting pills and a snack together for her."

"Don't mention it." Johannes disappeared up the stairs.

Emotion flooded Audrey's heart and warmed her. She gazed into Max's sea-blue eyes. "There aren't any guarantees. We're still at war for our very survival. But I'd rather have even a short time with you than be by myself forever. I feel our mate bond." She tapped her breastbone. "It burns like a beacon inside me, so bright you probably could have found us that way—if you'd been close enough."

"Devon and I talked about it. The problem was by the time we discovered you and Kate weren't where you were supposed to be, your captors had moved you beyond the range where that sort of thing works."

"I suppose, being shifters, they would've known that and put distance between us on purpose."

"Well," Max answered thoughtfully, "they wouldn't have realized we were mated, but they did know about Devon and Kate."

She swayed against him. "Guess I'm more tired than I thought. I'll see you upstairs."

"You won't have to wait long. After what happened today, I'm not letting you out of my sight for more than five minutes." He cupped a hand possessively around her ass. "Take a couple of whatever Johannes left by our door and drink the milk."

"Yes, Daddy."

"I'm not your father, although he seems like a hell of a nice guy."

Max tipped her chin up with his index finger and kissed her. He sank his tongue inside her mouth, and desire ignited in her belly. She reached between them and curled her fingers around his erect cock.

Max broke their kiss. "Uh-uh, none of that until you're better." He turned her around gently. "Up the stairs with you."

Audrey mounted the risers. Happiness spilled through her.

Maybe, if we're really careful and I'm on top, we can make love before we fall asleep.

The thought brought a smile to her face as she opened the door to her new bedroom—the one she shared with her mate. Bending carefully, she picked up the tray Johannes had left and carried it inside.

A *week later...*

Audrey sailed down the stairs. Max would be home soon, and she wanted to help Johannes with their dinner before he got there. She flexed her back. It was nearly healed, thanks to her wolf and spending a few days shifted.

"I still can't get over how fast your energy healed us."

"You're welcome. I didn't think you should shift so soon, but Max convinced me you'd heal faster once you found your wolf form. It wasn't as if you had stitches to rip out."

Audrey snorted. *"It sure felt that way when I shifted three days after we got back here."*

"Sorry. It hurt me too, but it was for the best."

"We had fun running around the estate grounds after dark. I love being a wolf."

Her wolf made a whuffling sound. *"That's because it's your destiny."*

Audrey pushed the swinging door into the kitchen open. "Hi, what can I do?"

Johannes turned from where he was chopping vegetables on the granite countertop. "We're having grilled salmon and vegetables, along with a salad."

"I'll whip up that yummy marinade you make for the grilled items."

He smiled. "Getting restless?"

She rolled her eyes and got a mixing bowl from one of the cupboards. "Yeah, my back is healed enough. I need to get back to work."

Johannes handed her sesame oil, balsamic vinegar, and some spices. "I thought you gave notice."

"I did. Max talked me out of it."

"Makes sense. I can see that he'd want you in a spot where either he or I can keep an eye on you."

She poured ingredients into the bowl, grabbed a whisk from a drawer, and beat the mixture until it was frothy. "It's more than that. I want to help the underground. Max convinced me I'd be more effective working undercover just like he does. No one saw my resignation but him, so I don't have to resurrect any bridges. We'll have to be careful, though, that no one at work finds out about our relationship. That sort of thing is frowned upon. I would have to quit then."

"Here." He pushed a large platter with raw salmon and zucchini, onion, and broccoli cut into wedges. "I'm glad you're better. It's been a long week."

"You could've come out to play with us at night," she said, referring to the moonlight romps she and Max had indulged in as wolves.

He frowned and shook his head. "No. I couldn't. One of us needed to be human in case there was trouble." His stern expression softened. "Not that I wouldn't have wanted to. Sometimes I fear I'll never find a mate since I don't spend any time as a mountain cat."

He sounded so wistful, it tugged at her heartstrings. "Max and I found one another without being shifted."

"You were incredibly lucky. You got to know one another working side-by-side, so you learned to respect and trust each other. And then you were gutsy enough to chase down the serum. Without that, Max would still be as mate-less as me."

"Aw." She poured the marinade over the fish and vegetables and stepped to his side. Audrey put her arms around him. "I'm sure it's just a matter of time. Once we get that edict repealed, there will be hot and cold shifter babes vying for your affection."

"Thanks! Only problem with your theory is they weren't hanging around before the edict, so I'm not terribly hopeful." He hugged her back and turned to get salad makings from the refrigerator.

Deep in her pocket, her wrist computer vibrated. Audrey dug it out and glanced at the ID for the incoming call. "Hmm… I don't recognize the number."

"Let me see." Johannes snatched it from her hand, scowling. He pushed *Answer* and then activated the speaker. "Yes. Can I help you?"

"Isn't this Audrey's computer code?" a male voice asked.

"It's Daddy," Audrey squealed and grabbed the wrist computer back. "Dad. Where are you?"

Ron didn't answer her question. Instead, he asked one of his own. "Was that Max? It didn't sound like him."

"Lord preserve me from overprotective males," she exclaimed. "It was Johannes. We're waiting for Max to get home from work. Are you close by?"

"Yes, dear," her mother cut in. "According to the car's nav system, we're about ten minutes from you."

"Wonderful! We'll make extra for dinner," Audrey said. "Love you guys. See you soon."

Johannes had already taken another package of fish out of the freezer and was cutting the plastic wrapper away. "I can nuke this," he said. "It will grill with everything else."

"Do we have extra veggies?"

He nodded. "In the fridge. If you could cut them up, it would be great."

"Dessert?"

"Any requests, madam?"

Audrey laughed. "You're getting to know me too well. I'd love another of your soufflés. They're scrumptious."

"I'll assemble it, if you could take over with the rest of dinner. Grill's already going." He gestured toward what had been a fireplace in the old-fashioned kitchen. Some previous owner had built a gas barbeque into it.

"Our mated one is close," her wolf crowed.

Audrey dialed into her lupine senses. Max was, indeed, closing on them. She grinned as she chopped more vegetables and added them to the platter.

"I recognize that look." Johannes grinned back. "Must mean Max will be here soon. All your lovemaking has driven me mad." His nose crinkled. "The house reeks of sex. I don't remember when I've jacked off so much."

"We'll just have to find you—"

Max swept through the kitchen door, made a beeline for Audrey, and pulled her against him. "What do we need to find Johannes?" he inquired just before he kissed her.

When she could talk again, she murmured. "A mate." Audrey wriggled out of his arms. "You feel divine, and I'd love to drag you upstairs and ravish you, but Mom and Dad will be here any moment."

Max sprinted for the front of the house. "Got to turn the lights on for them," he called over one shoulder.

AUDREY SAT BACK in her chair. Like everything that emerged from Johannes's kitchen, dinner had been a success. Her mother winked at her from across the table. "Thanks for pounding some sense into your father's cronies."

"Let's be fair," Ron cut in. "I'd been trying to *pound some sense* into them for months."

"I know," Bethea Westen said placatingly. "The problem was that you were only one voice. You needed reinforcements."

Max smiled winningly at her. "I know where Audrey gets her stunning good looks."

Bethea colored and touched red-blonde hair that curled around her face. "Thank you. That's quite a compliment."

"What?" Ron, who was seated next to his wife, turned to face her. "You never believed me when I told you how gorgeous you are? I was so pleased when Audrey got your eyes and your, um, build."

"Enough already." Bethea shook her head. "If one of you could show me where we'll be staying, I'll get our things laid out." She hesitated. "I know it's getting late, but you need to talk shifter business. Ron mentioned a few things driving up from the Bay Area."

"I'll take you." Johannes got to his feet and held out an arm. "I can help with your suitcases too."

"I just love how all of you are so courtly and old-world," Bethea murmured as he led her from the room.

Max set his dessert spoon down. "Anyone for brandy, port, or a cordial?"

"Whatever you're having," Ron said.

"I wouldn't mind some port," Audrey said. "I'll get it. You and Max can talk." She stood, went to the antique sideboard where the crystal stemware and liquor were kept, and gathered glasses and a bottle of twenty-year-old port. She poured snifters and passed them around.

"How'd things go after I left?" Max asked without preamble. He took a sip of port and rolled it around his mouth before swallowing.

Ron shrugged. "About how you'd expect. Some argued against what we'd hammered out." He nodded at Johannes as he returned to the dining room and slid into his chair.

Audrey pointed to the port and raised an eyebrow. When he nodded, she poured him a glass before she sat.

"The net effect?" Max asked.

"A few will remain in hiding but only about a dozen."

Max blew out a tense-sounding breath. "And the other splinter groups?"

"That plan is intact. We've already been in contact. The underground should start hearing from them within the next few days."

"I'm going back to the office next week," Audrey said. "Sounds as if things will be really busy."

"Are you certain you're well enough?" Max and Ron asked practically in unison.

"Not that it hasn't been hell without you," Max added diplomatically, "but—"

"I'm more than well enough," she broke in. "I could've worked today. Maybe yesterday too." She infused enough steel into her voice to make both men back down. "Christ! Being raised by a shifter father was bad enough. Now that there are two of you, I can see where I won't have a moment's peace."

"Oh, don't worry," Johannes said airily. "If they slack off, I'll dive into the breach."

Max started to laugh.

"I'm sure I don't see what's so funny," Audrey began before a giggle emerged. In moments, everyone was laughing.

"That's probably enough for tonight. I'm off to bed. We can strategize more in the morning." Ron stood.

"Second floor, right off the—" Johannes began.

Ron waved him to silence. "If the day comes when I can't find my wife using my sense of smell, I don't deserve to be a shifter anymore."

"Of course. Sorry," Johannes murmured.

"Good night, Daddy." Audrey got to her feet and went to him. She stood on her tiptoes and kissed him. "I'm glad you're here. Tell Mom I'm looking forward to spending time with her."

"I will, princess." Ron turned and left the room.

Audrey met Max's gaze from across the table. He was on his feet in an instant and by her side. "Bed for us too." Lust blazed from his eyes.

"We should help Johannes clean up the dinner things," she protested weakly.

"Go on." Johannes made shooing motions with both hands. "It's better if there's lots of real estate between us when the two of you get your hands on one another. As it is, I'm half-crazed with jealousy."

"You heard the man." Max held the door open for her.

Desire, sharp and poignant, knifed through her. Audrey didn't argue. At the bottom of the stairs, she spun and wrapped her arms around Max. "I love you."

"Not as much as I love you." He bent his head and kissed her.

Audrey opened her mouth beneath his, delighted by his probing tongue. Suddenly the two flights of stairs seemed like much too far, and she pushed her body against his, levering him into the dim recesses of the downstairs hall.

He ripped his mouth from hers. "Our bedroom's the other way."

"Don't you want to christen every room?" she inquired archly and ground her hips against his erection. Without waiting for an answer, she pushed the nearest door open. It led to a plush room lined with leather sofas and bookshelves. Moonlight spilled through leaded glass panes.

She kicked off her shoes, rucked her skirts up around her waist, and bent over an ottoman.

"No panties. Love the view." Max's words held the gravelly undercurrent that meant he was aroused past the point of restraint. A deep, decidedly male noise underscored his words, followed by the sound of a zipper.

His cock probed for entrance and she rotated her hips to give him a better angle. Her wolf wanted out. Sex from the rear was her position, but Audrey had gotten better at controlling when she shifted.

"You had lots of fun last night when we played outside," she reminded her bond animal.

Max snorted. "Yeah, my wolf is raising hell too. Guess we'll have to go outside—"

"Afterward," she cut in. "You know what I like. Give it to me."

"Why, darling. Who would've guessed my demure secretary was a closet dominatrix?"

"Stop talking and fuck me."

"Your wish is my command."

He slammed himself to the hilt, and she groaned with delight. Max did know exactly what she liked. They'd fucked so much in the time they'd been together, it amazed and delighted her. She butted her hips back against his pelvis, and he gripped her waist before starting the long, slow strokes that drove her beyond pleasure to a place where her climaxes crowded atop one another.

He swelled inside her, much like he did when they coupled in wolf form, and everything turned to scorching, liquid heat. Max snaked a hand between her legs and rubbed her swollen clit. It was all she needed to tumble off the cliff into an orgasm that rocked her to her core. Her heart pounded, and breath hitched in her throat. He rubbed harder and upped the tempo fucking her.

Body trapped between his ridged flesh and fingers, she tipped from one climax into the next and the next. Somewhere in between, she felt him release inside her, heard his satisfied cries, and tightened around him to maximize his delight. He closed his teeth over her shoulder, biting.

"Let me out," her wolf demanded. *"Now."*

"Soon."

Max pulled out of her body and sank to the floor, turning her and drawing her into his arms. "You're such a delight, my love."

She cuddled against him, sated, happy to be stealing borrowed moments of joy. Stroking the austere planes of his face, she murmured. "Feel like a romp through the grounds? We owe it to our animals."

"Right you are." After a lingering kiss, he got to his feet and pulled her upright. "You couldn't have known, but this room has an outside door that leads to the arboretum."

"I wondered why you had a second library. Is it to make it easier to take reading material outside?"

"There are far more than two. Before everything turned electronic, books were the only method for sharing knowledge. I have a lot of them. Far more than a single room or two could hold." He shinnied out of his clothes and inclined his head. "After you, darling."

Audrey tugged her top over her head, unfastened her skirt, letting it pool around her feet, and reached for her wolf. It crashed into her with shocking speed, and she took off through the door Max held open.

The air glistened as he shifted, his white pelt gleaming in the moonlight. They raced to the end of the yard, sat back on their haunches, and howled at the moon.

"I'm so happy." Audrey licked Max's snout.

"If I have anything to say about it, you always will be." He licked her back, and they leaned into one another before he took off at a dead run with her in hot pursuit.

THIS IS the end of *Wolf Born*. Read on for a sample from *Blood Bond*, conclusion to the Underground Heat Series. Johannes finds a mate, but the price is high.

ABOUT THE AUTHOR

Ann Gimpel is a USA Today bestselling author. A lifelong aficionado of the unusual, she began writing speculative fiction a few years ago. Since then her short fiction has appeared in a number of webzines and anthologies. Her longer books run the gamut from urban fantasy to paranormal romance. Once upon a time, she nurtured clients, now she nurtures dark, gritty fantasy stories that push hard against reality. When she's not writing, she's in the backcountry getting down and dirty with her camera. She's published over 50 books to date, with several more planned for 2018 and beyond. A husband, grown children, grandchildren and wolf hybrids round out her family.

Keep up with her at www.anngimpel.com or http://anngimpel.blogspot.com

If you enjoyed what you read, get in line for special offers and pre-release special reads. Sign up for Ann's newsletter on her website or her blog.

Keep reading for a teaser from *Blood Bond!*

BLOOD BOND, CHAPTER ONE

Johannes Takes wandered from the kitchen to the cozy study with its forbidden fireplace burning real, but equally forbidden, logs. Thank Christ for catalytic elements that all but obliterated any trace of smoke from the air outside. He eyed an overstuffed chair, but was too keyed up to sit, so he clasped his hands behind his back and watched the fire. The oblivion he sought eluded him, though.

Thoughts he usually kept tightly leashed pressed hard against his habitually imposed restraint. It was best when he kept his feelings buried, so they couldn't get in the way and trip him up. He moved closer to the fire, holding out his hands to its warmth. His people faced grave challenges. Trials that could mean the death of many, many shifters. Nothing less than his absolute attention to every single detail would do. There had to be a way through their current difficulties, but he was damned if he saw a clear road.

Beyond the threat of genocide for his kin, personal demons badgered him.

While he was delighted Max Sigayev and Audrey Westen were mated—and it had been an honor to be the one joining them—still their joy underscored his loneliness. He and Max went back close to two hundred years. They'd met in a very different time, a time when finding clean air and water wasn't a problem. A time when shifters were valued and could walk free with their heads high.

Not anymore.

Thanks to a U.S. government edict, copied by every other industrialized nation, shifters had become persona non grata. Reviled. Shunned. Rounded up and killed.

Johannes curled his hands into fists so hard his nails cut into his palms. Maybe because he'd been around for virtually all of Max's life, the other shifter hadn't ever asked him very many questions about himself. Johannes's vague replies about working in espionage had been accurate enough—and they'd satisfied Max's curiosity.

What he'd left out was that his original employer had been Odysseus.

Johannes was the first shifter, created by Ceres, guardian of the earth, and he was immortal. A corner of his mouth twisted downward. He'd been an experiment. The goddess kept the shifter part, but decided the earth would quickly become overpopulated if none of them ever died, so subsequent shifters weren't dealt the immortal card.

He'd faded in and out of sight over his better than two thousand years of existence. Shifters were long lived, but nothing like him. In truth, his relationship with Max and the shifter underground were the closest he'd come to permanence in a very long time. Ceres had made it abundantly clear he wasn't to tell anyone about the extra gift she'd given him.

And he never had.

Johannes sank into a squat before the flames and shook his head. Gift, his ass. More like a curse. Since he couldn't tell anyone, it had limited his congress with women to sex. Lots of it with a variety of intriguing partners, but he'd always run like hell if he started to care. Even absent finding his mated one—which hadn't happened—he'd been afraid to fall in love, knowing he'd have to watch the woman die, and then the next one, and the next.

"Oh for Christ fucking sake," he muttered and pushed to his feet.

Looking back never did any good, never yielded different answers. Just the same old, tired details.

Maybe a walk in the moonlight would help. He pushed open a side door and engaged his mountain cat senses, sniffing. Max and Audrey had been out here—and not very long ago—but they were back inside. He grabbed a jacket off a hook and slipped into it to cut the chill of the winter night.

The old mansion he and Max had purchased sat in one of Sacramento's older neighborhoods on a generous piece of land. They'd bought it years before—just like they'd bought real estate all around the globe to assure they had choices, in case they couldn't remain in a particular location. The place had remained empty until Max came up with his harebrained scheme to run for California governor. Max was so certain he'd win, he'd begun shipping things from one of their many European manor houses to furnish this one months before the election.

"Harebrained, but brave," Johannes's mountain cat commented from his permanent spot in Johannes's mind.

"Can't fault him for lacking guts." Johannes grinned, but his smile faded fast. *"Haven't heard much from you lately. Do you have any ideas for how we play out the endgame?"*

"You called a spade a spade," the cat said quietly. *"Whatever happens over the next few weeks will determine the outcome of the war humans are waging against us."*

"You didn't exactly answer me." Johannes made his way to a good-sized pond and watched ripples in the water from koi that swam in its depths.

"Too many variables. Since we have no idea what the opposition will do next, it makes it hard to plan. We also don't know if all the shifter splinter groups will join our effort."

Bending, Johannes selected a flat rock and skipped it over the pond's surface. The sad truth was not all the rogue shifters would join the underground, and those that didn't would end up cannon fodder—murdered by one side or the other. He'd seen that particular scenario play itself out many times.

It made him sad—and angry—but there wasn't much he could do to alter it. The sound of one of the house doors snicking open caught at his sensitive feline hearing. Who the hell could it be? Surely not Max and Audrey, who were likely locked in one more heated embrace.

He rolled his eyes and trotted toward the far side of the house where he'd heard the door open. Shifters loved sex—lived for it— and mated sex was the best there was, yielding an inexhaustible well of passion. Another of Ceres's gifts, she'd substituted pleasure for immortality.

Audrey's mother, Bethea Westen, walked a few paces from the house. When she saw him, she came to a halt. "Sorry. Guess I wasn't the only one who couldn't sleep."

She met his gaze with hazel eyes a lot like Audrey's. Bethea looked like a slightly older version of her daughter, with curly strawberry-blonde hair and a tall, curvaceous figure. Tonight she was wrapped in a black, wool coat that almost scraped the ground.

"You're worried about emerging from hiding." Johannes stated it as fact because he was practically certain it was true.

Bethea nodded. "Of course. Who wouldn't be?" She hesitated. "It's more than that, though. Ron thinks there will be fighting. Lots of it." Tears sheened her eyes, but she didn't brush them aside. "I know most of you shifters don't take me seriously because I'm only a human, but I love Ron. I don't think I could stand it if anything happened to him, and me telling him to leave the rough stuff for the younger ones gets me nowhere. As shifters go, he is young."

Johannes wasn't certain what to say. He didn't want to lie. Besides, she wouldn't believe him anyway, so he maintained a supportive silence.

"Sorry. I didn't mean to say that much. It just sort of slipped out." Bethea turned to go.

"The yard is big enough for us both," Johannes said. "Don't let me chase you back inside."

She eyed him. "Where are you from?"

"Why would you ask?"

A sheepish smile curved her lips. "Guess it wasn't very polite of me, but I was trying to figure it out over dinner. Sometimes you sound German. Sometimes Austrian. There were even a few times when you had a hint of a Russian accent like Max, though his speech is pretty purely American most of the time."

"I've lived a long time in a lot of different places," he murmured.

"Yes, but where were you from originally?" she persisted. "Unless you don't want to tell me, which is all right too."

He smiled back. What could the harm be? "Greece," he said. "I was born in Greece."

"Really?" She sharpened her gaze, and her intensity reminded him a lot of Audrey. "I never would've guessed."

"You'd be in good company. Not many do."

"You're part of the underground's security force, aren't you?"

He quested for a noncommittal response. "You might say that."

"So you're a good one to ask. What do you think will happen with Ron and the others emerging from hiding and joining up with the underground?"

Seems like the question of the hour tonight.

"I wish I had a solid answer for you, but there are too many unknowns. Once we see how many shifters we have to work with, we'll be able to determine what kind of offensive strategy might work." He paused for a beat. "The other alternative—but it's much weaker to my way of thinking—is to defend ourselves against whatever they throw our way."

Bethea furrowed her forehead, clearly considering his words. "But won't you do that anyway? Defend yourselves from attack, I mean?"

"Of course. I didn't explain myself very well. The best campaigns are a combination of offense and defense."

Her next words came slowly. "I guess no one would be exempt. No shifters, anyway."

"The more who join the cause, the more likely we'll prevail." Johannes forged ahead before she could say more. "I can't believe you like the way you've lived these past two years. Skulking about. Living on throwaways and whatever else you could scrounge. It's no way to craft a life."

"Ron and the others were sure this would all blow over—at the beginning."

"Except it just got worse. We didn't form the underground immediately. Only after they started rounding us up and throwing us in prison."

"I guess that's what happens when you give in to bullies." Her voice was soft. "It encourages them to do even worse to you."

"You're right." Johannes had balled his hands into fists, and he flexed his fingers to relax the tension thrumming through his body. "I tell you this, madam. We will win this. Shifters deserve to survive. We hold magic that has the power to enrich everyone's lives. Earth would be a grim place without us."

He stopped shy of launching into the myth about Ceres searching for her daughter and how it spawned the cold, bitter seasons. Even though gods and goddesses were long absent from view, he had no doubt they still existed. What would Ceres do if shifters—her creation—were wiped out?

He had a feeling her retribution would be swift and brutal. And since he was the only one who couldn't die, he'd at least get to witness it.

"Madam, huh?" Bethea's voice broke into his thoughts. "Your Old Country roots are showing. I have a feeling there're things you're not saying—"

The side door Bethea had used swung open, and Ron loped to his wife's side. "There you are. What are you doing outside bothering Johannes?"

"She's not bothering me," Johannes said. "We were having an interesting philosophical discussion."

Ron snorted. "Yeah. I'll bet. She was probably out here trying to figure out a way to talk you into making certain I end up with a desk job in whatever crapola the humans throw our way next."

"No, she actually wasn't. She is worried, but it's only because she loves you." Johannes blew out a breath. "I'm going back inside. If the two of you want to walk through the grounds, they're quite safe."

Without waiting for them to answer, he slipped past and strode around the mansion to the door into the study. The fire was burning low, but he didn't feed it. Time to turn in. He didn't sleep much, but maybe if he rested his eyes and body he'd come up with a better plan to deal with the shit storm heading their way.

Humans had good intel, and they had to know about the influx of shifters swelling the underground's ranks. He picked up a bottle of Madeira and a snifter and walked slowly upstairs. Max lived in a suite at one end of the third floor. Johannes occupied the entirety of the fourth.

In front of the door leading to his rooms, he tipped his chin so the retinal scanner could read him. The locking mechanism ticked open, and he walked into the large, open space he'd crafted to please his aesthetic needs—and those of his cat. Because his living space took up the entire floor, every wall was lined with windows.

Johannes liked it that way. Both the sunrise and sunset glittered through leaded glass panes. At the moment, they framed an almost full moon. A large bed butted into one corner. An even larger desk littered with myriad computer gadgetry sat across from it. Above the electronics, a wall-sized screen blinked with messages and intelligence gathered from around the world by Johannes's many connections. Bookshelves ran from the bottom of the windows to the floor, overflowing with books and scrolls. A veritable fortune in antiquarian books graced his shelves, and he used many of them as ongoing resource materials. Nothing even remotely akin to them were available through the vid feed. Libraries had thinned out years before. No one had the funds to maintain very many of them.

He kicked off his shoes and removed the jacket he'd plucked from downstairs. It actually belonged to Max, so he should return it, but he'd do that tomorrow. Not much remained of the night as it was. He pulled his sweater over his head, draped it over a chair, and unfastened his trousers. In between getting undressed, he poured himself half a snifter of the Madeira and sipped, savoring its exotic, spicy scent.

Once he was nude, he wrapped himself in a robe and padded into the bathroom at the far end of his suite. Open like the rest of the space, it hosted a highly illegal deep soaking tub made of creamy, red-veined marble. The government had outlawed tubs years ago since they wasted water. Johannes controlled data flowing into and out of the mansion, so masking water use was easy enough to finesse. Not that he was into wasting resources, but he did enjoy the occasional soak. The floor was rare, ivory-toned slate imported from Ceylon. In truth, it was more of an indulgence than the tub.

He killed the Madeira and thought about a bath. In the end, he settled for a shower, letting the body jets from the wall mounted unit pummel him as he soaped and rinsed. The water had a stimulating effect—not quite what he was hoping for—and his penis swelled.

Johannes shut the shower off and grabbed a fluffy dark brown towel. Everything had a *stimulating* effect since Max and Audrey's lust made the house smell like an upscale bordello to his sensitive nose. His cock twitched to full attention, curved against his belly. He tried to ignore it, but sensation coursed through him, along with a visual of the last woman he'd fucked.

Finding partners was easy. Shifters held an easy grace, and humans were desperately attracted to them. All he had to do was wander into any bar or shop or restaurant, and women practically threw themselves at him. Sometimes, if they smelled appealing to him and his cat agreed, he took them up on their offered delights.

Curving a hand around his ridged flesh, he gave in to desire heating his blood. A woman was better than his hand, but right now he wanted expediency, and he wouldn't be clear-headed until after he came.

He moved from the bathroom to a thick Oriental carpet covering hardwood flooring and sat down, resting his back against the end of his bed. A flick of his wrist brought the wall screen to life. A few more adjustments, and one of his favorite fantasies flared to life.

A stunning Asian with long, straight dark hair that kissed her hips waltzed straight toward him and stopped, legs slightly spread. Small, conical breasts with peaked nipples teased him. He'd built the simulation, so it met his sexual needs perfectly.

"Johannes." The woman ran her tongue over full lips, and her dark eyes glittered with lust. "I've missed you." She stroked her hands down the clean lines of her body and shoved her hair aside, baring everything for him.

He decided which of several voice-activated programs he wanted and asked, "What have you missed?"

In this simulation, it would be just her. Others included more women and even another man or two.

"This." She closed a hand over one breast, tweaking and twirling her nipple. "And this." She dipped her other hand between her legs, tilting her pelvis, so he could watch her masturbate.

As she teased her breasts, and rubbed her clit in hard, little circles, he tightened his hold around his cock, adding some saliva to lubricate things. Asian girl moaned, and her skin developed a rosy hue as her excitement mounted. Johannes pinched his nipples to heighten his sensation and jacked himself hard. He and Asian girl had done this enough, he could time his climax to almost exactly match hers.

"Tell me." His voice was taut with lust.

"I know. Tell you when I'm almost there." She shut her eyes and rubbed herself harder. In a single, fluid motion she bent to one side and picked up a dildo.

Even though he knew what would happen next, he never tired of watching her stretch full length on a plush futon and slide the fake cock inside her. She positioned her legs so he could watch her fuck herself, and when she pulled the dildo out, it glistened with her secretions. One hand manipulated the sex toy; the other traded between her breasts and her clit.

"Yes, Johannes. Close." She looked right at him because that was how he'd programmed it. Her nipples were hard buds, and her golden skin glowed with desire.

He tweaked his nipples again and jacked himself harder, faster. His balls tightened, and he reached behind them, pressing the spot that always made him wild with lust.

Asian girl was panting, gasping for air. Her eyes flicked open. "Now," she shouted. "Come now."

Almost as if the hologram had power, semen bubbled from his balls and shot from his cock in sheets of delight. His hips pumped and writhed, and he sucked air, maximizing every shred of pleasure as his cock juddered in his hand.

"That was wonderful. Let's do it again soon." Asian girl winked lazily, and the screen shaded to blackness.

"You've turned that into an art form," his cat noted wryly. *"How about finding us a shifter to fuck?"*

Johannes struggled to normalize his breathing. Guilt smote him. Holograms added spice to his non-existent love life, but they did less than nothing for his cat. Sure, it came whenever he did, but it knew the simulation—and stimulation—wasn't real.

Hell, he knew it wasn't real too, but it was better than nothing, and it hadn't taken him much time to build the various programs he used to jack off with.

I'm making excuses.

"Sorry," he told his cat. *"Maybe with all the shifters coming out of hiding, our mate will show up."*

"You know that's not true." His cat's voice held a different note, one Johannes hadn't heard before.

"What do you mean?"

"There's no mated one for us. We're the only immortal shifter bondmates in the entire universe."

The cat's sadness reverberated inside Johannes, but he tried to soothe his bond animal. *"Just because there might not be a mated one for us is no reason we can't enjoy sex with a shifter."*

"We can. And we have. But what's the point? I appreciate you trying to make me feel better, but I'm done talking for now. I withdraw my request for you to find us a shifter for sex."

Johannes got to his feet, grabbed a towel, and cleaned up his mess. As usual, his cat cut to the heart of things. They might find a shifter to have sex with—or even fall in love—but the magic of the mate bond would always elude them. If it hadn't knocked on their door in better than two thousand years, it never would.

"Enough." He spoke aloud to force himself to move forward.

A quick glance at his mostly unopened messages convinced him they could wait. Too many to deal with, and he was tired. Closing eyes for half an hour would help his concentration. He threw himself face down on the bed and was asleep almost before his head hit the pillow.

Frantic pounding on his door dragged him awake. A gray dawn flickered through the windows as he thrust the muzziness of sleep aside. He'd obviously done more than nap. The pounding escalated.

What the fuck?

Claws poked through his fingers, but he held his cat back. *"Not yet. We don't know what's wrong."*

www.ingramcontent.com/pod-product-compliance
Lightning Source LLC
Chambersburg PA
CBHW071802190726
48292CB00008B/2682